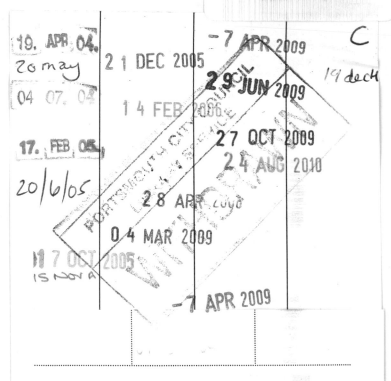

This book is due for return by the last date shown above.
To avoid paying fines please renew or return promptly

Portsmouth
CITY COUNCIL
LIBRARY SERVICE   CL-1

First published in the UK in 2003 by
Dewi Lewis Publishing
8 Broomfield Road
Heaton Moor
Stockport SK4 4ND
+44 (0)161 442 9450

www.dewilewispublishing.com

ISBN: 1-899235-64-7

Design & artwork production: Dewi Lewis Publishing
Printed and bound in Great Britain by
Biddles Ltd, Guildford and King's Lynn

3   5   7   9   8   6   4   2

First Edition

Homesickness

a novel by

Helen E. Mundler

DEWI LEWIS
PUBLISHING

Or, Polar Expedition, Ill-Equipped

To Marc Lévy, and Roman

Long did I foolishly think that there were images of
Vesta: afterwards I learned that there are none
under her carved dome.

Ovid

'Et maintenant, tu dois aller chercher quelque chose?'
'Non. Pas pour le moment.'
Elle me souriait. Elle s'était aperçue, sans doute,
que je me moquais gentiment d'elle. Les valises, le
manteau de fourrure, le chien... Aujourd'hui je
comprends mieux ces allées et venues pour tenter de
rassembler les morceaux épars d'une vie.

Patrick Modiano

The true adventuress knows she can never
go home again.

Anita Brookner

Prologue

Even now I have to wonder periodically whether I could go back, to project the scene in my mind: the homecoming. I know by heart what I felt every time I really went, and what I'd still feel now – first the reluctance of the child treated babyishly, the humiliation of giving in, too old, to the soft enveloping of the maternal breast. And then the helpless knowledge that I could never, of my own volition, leave.

And yet once there, always, the failure to engage. Alice in Wonderland grown too big for her room, elbows and shoulders struggling against tight confines. Hiding frigidly behind the semblance of politeness. I think how it would be with someone else, with you, dreamed receiver of this unsent letter. The moment looked forward to from the day of planning the trip or even before, still from the last time, still from the moment of the first parting: 'Papa!' I throw my bags down on the rainy ground at the station, and bury my face in your shoulder, laughing and crying into your soft wool sweater, and you hold me tightly, kissing my hair. In the car we don't speak much, but, both smiling inwardly, we know how much we yearn, how empty has been the space between us, and the time. Home to papa. Hold me forever.

That is not how it can be. There is conversation, brittle-polite, to make up for a childhood of screamed impolitenesses, but my parents do not see me. Little is asked, in either sense. The barriers are insurmountable, the seals hermetic. The television, rationed and mistrusted in childhood, is quickly turned on. It is not simply that I have left, and that leaving was irrevocable, even before the final decision was made, even before I took my bags and shut the door and posted the key through the letter box, even before I failed to look back on my childhood home before going away for the last time, for fear, perhaps, of paralysis, a pillar of salt. No. There has been, somewhere, a more radical departure. The wound is deeper. And for a lifetime I may quest after liberty, the severing of the umbilical cord, but with this need, all the time, collides the impulse to return to the breast, the desire for succour; a yearning to lose the identity, the individuality, so hard won.

When the need to come back becomes absolute – and however far I go, for however long, there always comes a point when it does – in my dreams I take planes and cross-country trains and creep up the suburban driveway, a thief in the night with a secret roll of tools, and set about picking the locks. I enter very quietly, not to disturb the twilight hush of the house in summer, before I call: Mummy. Daddy. It's me. But where I longed for excited cries – Why didn't you let us know? – the silence continues eerie as I stray from room to room. The furniture has gone or it is stacked to be collected, cardboard boxes are packed and scatter floors, curtains have been removed. All remnants of childhood, every vestige of the past, stripped and sent, chastised, away. I make my echoing steps purposely louder as I progress, unable to give up the search, conscious of inevitable failure. Home cannot be gone back to. Did it ever exist? An illusion, something I believed in when I was small, and should long have managed to outgrow.

I open doors off the hall and light streams in from the garden, crepuscular, purplish, bruising. Two figures, stiff, looking towards old age and death, sit upright and staring on horsehair sofas. Frozen, unsmiling, unspeaking.

You have to let me come home. Mother. Father. If you don't, then who can possibly? If you don't, I will break in with pickaxes, time and time again. Look at me, speak to me, I want to cry, but it is clear that they cannot. Their eyes are glazed, unseeing. Answer me! React! Mother, why are you so cold? Father, I can't find a pulse! And the closer I look, the more your head seems to be made of papier mâché, and I can feel inside me – I can't stop – that I'm going to bat it off like a cat with a ping-pong ball, this ludicrous head, and it will fall and disintegrate, dust to dust.

And it takes more courage than I have to stand and confront these icy effigies, these empty rooms. I turn on my heel like a princess in a fairy tale gone bad, and flee for my life.

Ilona

I

There is a footstool placed against the chair which Dr Echs offers Ilona. She glances at it and he says, 'You can sit on the stool if you like'. This she does and looks down at the carpet, fiddling with the fastening of one shoe. He leans forward, the ends of his fingertips pressed together, trying to get her to look up, and says, gently, 'Do you know why you're here?' At this she shifts uneasily and the fair skin goes through scarlet to a deep wine red. She finds it appalling to have to tell him why, but there is also in her mind the fear of losing Daniel, the fear of his rejection. She says, almost too quietly for the doctor to hear, 'Because of what happens at night'. He can feel waves of fear and closure coming off her, and pulls his chair closer, but she shrinks further into herself and lets her hair fall forward, half-hiding her face. The closeness of the contact, although several feet of empty carpet still separate them, is unbearable to her. This half amuses Dr Echs because he can feel behind her reticence the desire to confide. But her blush is painful, and she starts to cry with sheer embarrassment, trapped in an impossible situation. He suggests they go into his office. He knows that she likes to draw so they sit down at the desk, and he gives her a piece of paper, a good soft pencil and a rubber, because he guesses she will want to make a workmanlike job of it, and asks her to draw the house at Ste Marie, so that she can tell him about it. He is interested to see that she draws it as a plan, the house represented as what goes on where, not a façade. She sketches her room, Daniel's, the kitchen, the veranda, the salon, the loft, and indicates directions from the back door with arrows, and then the pencil hovers above her own room. He helps her: where's your bed? what colour is the quilt? do you have any animals on your bed?

Ilona begins to talk, about her bear. This was the first thing that Daniel had given her, in Canada, picked up, as she little suspects, in haste and guilt at the airport on the outward journey, when he had been intending to come back home without her; a small ursine pay-off. An old-fashioned jointed bear, with slightly shaggy honey-coloured fur and a tartan bow at the neck, and paws that seemed to be real leather. As soon as she had received it, it had become to her

13

the visible manifestation of Daniel's love, or at least his intention to love, and she had sat it on her dressing table at Lily and Vic's – the neighbours with whom she had been staying – during the day, and taken it to bed at night. Without mentioning the bear to Daniel or thanking him more than once, she had shown an excessive fondness for it. She does not put it like this to Dr. Echs, but simply says that she had liked it.

'Then I cut it up.' He will get used to the abruptness of her narratives, the laconic statements, what he calls allusiveness and what she strongly feels is saying what she means. He is, he supposes, invited to prompt with questions.

'When was this? In Canada or in France? What did you cut it up with?'

Ilona says it was not long after her arrival at Ste Marie, that she had cut its stomach, all the way down, with the kitchen scissors, pulled the stuffing out and thrown the newly-flaccid bear across the room.

'How did Daniel react? Was he angry?'

Daniel had not been angry, he had been nonplussed. Ilona, appalled at her own barbarity, had sobbed, face down on her bed, and he had gathered up the kapok and stuffed it back into the opening, gone to find a needle and thread, and then made her turn over and look, see that it would be alright, that the damage was reparable. His stitches were large and not entirely straight, but he had told Ilona, who liked making things, that she could make him a t-shirt and cover up the damage. She had sobbed, I'm sorry, I'm sorry, over and over again.

'Why do you think you did it?' Dr Echs tries.

'I don't know. I wished I hadn't. I wish I hadn't.'

Did it occur to her, when she was doing it, that babies come out of mothers' stomachs?

Ilona says she doesn't know. When Dr Echs mentions the story to Daniel, he says that it had occurred to him.

'Aborting herself,' Daniel suggests. 'Am I that bad a mother?'

'So you see yourself as Ilona's mother?'

Daniel shrugs. 'What else?'

*

In the following session, Dr Echs tells Ilona, 'It can be a way for your body to express something that's going on in your mind that you find hard to talk about.' Another rush of colour rises, so he goes on, looking at the notes he's received from the paediatrician, and those taken from Daniel's account: 'It seems you're having difficulty eating. And that you – ran away, when you arrived in France with Daniel? Maybe you could tell me a little about that.'

Silence.

'It's all the same thing,' she attempts desperately. A pause and then, 'I just want my mother'. And the tears which at present are never very far begin again to sluice her cheeks.

This is such a pertinent observation that with anyone else he would have ended the session. But Ilona, whose weight is getting dangerously low, whose states of listlessness have been by all accounts almost catatonic, is within a hairsbreadth of hospitalisation, although she doesn't know this herself. He says, taking the risk of alienating her through further embarrassment: 'How did your mother react when you used to wet your bed, when you were younger?'

Still crying, she nonetheless thinks about this. 'Like Daniel', she says after a pause. 'She used to come and – ' she stammers over the shameful words, gives up – 'and then read me a story. Till I went back to sleep. She used to stroke my hair.'

'And is that what Daniel does?'

'He – he – '

A pause, but the effort is being made. 'He puts his arms round me.' Another attempt. 'On his lap.'

'And you like that?'

No words, just a nod. The tears have stopped. A sigh.

'How did Daniel find out? Did he catch you, did you tell him?'

'I told him. The first – as soon as he came. Then I felt stupid.' A pause of a different kind. He can feel her ready to launch. 'I didn't mean to tell him. I didn't know what to do. When he came I was in our house – not next door with Lily and Vic – I was looking for – I needed some – I couldn't find any – '

The narrative grinds to a halt. He says, 'What was it you were looking for?'

Ilona says desperately, 'I didn't know what to do with the sheets. I needed...' Silence again. 'When my mother was ill she stopped

15

coming in to me because she was taking tablets to make her sleep and then she wouldn't wake up. So she didn't know. And after she died it was like that at Lily and Vic's as well. So I had to use... towels.'

'Sanitary towels?'

She is not wholly sure that she knows what he means.

'Towels – from the airing cupboard – '

'I understand.'

She feels a little wave of peace settle over her, and knows that he does understand, although she will later be appalled at what she has said, at what she has been made to say.

'And what did you do with them? Wash them out?'

She shakes her head. 'I threw them away.'

*

Daniel has never imagined that a daughter could be a possible thing for him to have, a possible person to enter his life, but as he hovers above the Atlantic on the way to pick Ilona up from Vancouver, he recollects that Hestia was always determined to give him one. He has to find a way out.

Hestia is dead, very recently dead. A remarkable number of the people Daniel was once at college with are dead. Sven, once Daniel's closest friend, and biologically Ilona's father, killed himself eleven years ago, before she was born. His death is older than she is. David, someone to row with and drink with in Durham, later Daniel's lover, died two and a half years ago, victim to a random tourist killing, on the other side of the world, where he had gone to walk and to think. When he disappeared, it had taken the police six weeks to find his body, hidden in a cave. A vacant interlunar cave, Daniel thinks, now, always. He wonders frequently how long he took to die, whether he knew he was dying, alone. David was a doctor. If conscious, he would have understood what was happening to him, and fought.

Others have died in boats and on bicycles or falling from ladders, or, again, murdered.

Ilona is now ten, and Daniel has not seen her since she was six, when he stayed a few days in Vancouver. He has seen Hestia since on her occasional trips to Europe, unaccompanied because she doesn't like Ilona to live out of a suitcase, to be starved of sleep, to be uprooted. Hestia came, on the last of these trips, to say that there was a chance that she was dying. She didn't know how great a chance. In the end it wasn't chance mutating cells that killed her: she lost her life crossing a road. Her papers gave Daniel the legal right to adopt Ilona.

*

'Hestia used to say, she's practically yours anyway. Or she said it once.'

'What do you think she meant by that?' asks Dr Echs.

'She would have liked her to be mine. We were at university together, the three of us. Hestia, Sven, and I. I – felt quite strongly for Sven. Hestia – she used to say she loved me. Although she knew – . But Sven and Hestia were the only heterosexual pair in the triangle, and so they were the ones who – that was how Ilona was conceived. Hestia would have liked her to be mine. Through some sort of transfer of sperm.'

'But this didn't happen when you were at university? If Ilona is only ten now?'

'No, it was much later. Hestia came back to London. She'd been away for years, living abroad, a sort of self-imposed exile. She didn't have anywhere to go so I persuaded Sven to rent a room to her.'

'You couldn't have rented her a room yourself?'

'I was with David. We lived together. I don't think Hestia would have wanted it. She never learned to let go, not in all the years I knew her. So it was painful for her, to see us together. But we weren't very far away, just round the corner. We all saw a lot of each other.'

*

From what Daniel can remember now, and from the photos he has in his flight bag – a whole packet of beautiful photos sent by Hestia, perhaps as blackmail, parts of different series, taken recently but at different times – Ilona is thin and blonde, like Sven. Hestia has always said she is highly strung, that she has tried to make up for this

17

but has feared that her very presence perpetuates it. Daniel can remember Ilona aged one and just beginning to try to walk, and then at three, snuggling against his shoulder on the sofa when he stayed for ten days, letting him put her to bed, whispering 'I love you' in his ear, and appearing again, perched on his bed like a little imp, horribly early in the mornings, to talk to him. Waking afraid in the night and having to be soothed back to sleep. In that time, he has sent her sporadic postcards, and she has sent him first scribbles, then home-made cards, rather well-executed, at Christmas, but the rapidity of events has meant that there has been almost no transition from that state of affairs to now – when after staying in Canada for two weeks, for the funeral and to sort out Hestia's affairs, he is supposed to be taking Ilona home to live with him. No way, thinks Daniel, grimly. He is on his way to St Oswald to try to sort things out, to find a solution. He does not want a child; he does not want Hestia's daughter. There is no room in his life for this. He will not give in to blackmail, particularly emotional blackmail from beyond the grave; Hestia should have got her life in order before bowing out of it so hastily.

Nonetheless, within twelve hours of receiving the call from Lily, Hestia's next door neighbour and oddly ill-assorted friend and mainstay, from what he has gathered, he has boarded a plane from the south of France for Paris and then to Vancouver and St-Oswald.

Daniel thinks, he does not cease to think, that it has all happened very quickly. He intends to resist, staunchly. He will go and sort things out as best he can for Ilona, and then come home, alone. What the hell is he supposed to do with a child? A child half-made and orphaned, at the age of ten. Until Daniel got the last in the series of Hestia's calls from Canada, the real this-is-it, this-is-impending-death, call, he hadn't really believed it would happen.

He had been bludgeoned into agreeing years before that he would be responsible for the welfare of Hestia's child if anything happened to her, but here it is, happening, and even that period has tunnelled out of control to the point where it has happened, is already in the past. Hestia has made her arrangements and died, packed a weekend case and departed this existence, leaving her affairs in the hands of others. It has not been established what she intended – she had written so much, creatively and otherwise, about suicide. But the fact is that following letters, faxes, phone calls, she went to Vancouver, saw her lawyer, and walked down in to the street and under a car, which could have been shock, or drowsiness, or a sudden access of despair, or a planned avoidance of a lingering hospital death. Or of saying goodbye to Ilona. When Hestia left Ilona the previous morning, Ilona will tell him, she hugged and kissed her tenderly, but then she was that kind of mother. She believed in demonstrative and demonstrable love.

Thus death came or seemed to come not in a crescendo but in a single bang, and Daniel had realised he would have to leave immediately, to get himself on a plane, to comfort his unwillingly inherited child, and somehow to make arrangements for her future. On impulse at the airport he bought the bear, visited in spite of himself by a memory of Ilona as a very little girl, telling him, in a sudden burst of confidentiality, about the furry rabbits without which she could not sleep. He sits, now, with a hand squeezed around the bear's belly as he waits in the departure lounge, not reading the paper he has bought, suddenly very apprehensive about what he has to do. He has said nothing to anybody else of his intentions, or lack of them. There is a lot to be made clear, but he is a lawyer, with a good line in insidious understatement, and he has no qualms about his ability to do so.

By the time Daniel arrives, mid-morning, Ilona has been sitting in her mother's bedroom for a good hour, stroking Lily's black cat, Polly, who has made for herself a little hollow on the double bed where she crouches, flattened and purring. Ilona has chosen to await Daniel here, in a place that belongs to her, while Lily, next door, tries anxiously not to survey. Vic has gone to the airport to pick Daniel up and will drop him off speedily before going on to his office; he is a notary. There are things on Ilona's mind, between her and the cliff-edge of pain which has just opened up. Lily has said to her, I expect you were too young to remember much about Daniel. This is singularly untrue. There are certain memories that Ilona cherishes, which, pulled up on the mind's screen, induce a pleasurable shame, making her turn at night and hide her face from herself in her pillow.

*

'What do you remember about your first meeting with Ilona? Did you like her, how did you feel about her?'

It is Dr. Echs who asks the question.

*

It was morning. An odd time to arrive. The whole day lay ahead, impossible to bury the event in social flurry, get it over, have a meal and go to bed, a long night for each player to consider the terrain and marshal his or her defences for the next day. Daniel, dropped at the house by Vic, had been asked whether he would like to go inside, have coffee, settle in, but had been told that Ilona was in the house next door. He felt he owed her a clear statement of the facts, immediately, that she should know the score.

'Upstairs, I think,' said Lily.

Ilona has clearly been waiting for him, for his arrival from France, for the two days since he was summoned, with hungry anticipation. She is in her mother's bedroom, empty because her mother is dead, on the edge of the bed, stroking the black cat's ears. The cat is no longer purring. The front door has been left on the latch and Daniel enters, leaving his bags in the hall, listens, hesitates, and then starts quietly up the stairs. Ilona? There is a tense, breathing silence. Ilona's eyes are fixed on the floor, her heart is pounding, the situation is utterly unmanageable. The cat, sensing tension, pours herself neatly off the bed and slinks away. Daniel, going forward, feels relief at the withdrawal of this witness. He comes towards the child, crouches in front of her, takes her cold hand and looks into her face and says, this time aloud, 'Ilona?' He has his speech prepared. He will do everything he can for her, but it is quite impossible that she should come and live with him; he will come over and see her twice a year, there will be phone calls, letters, birthday presents.

She still won't look up, her hair, thick and blonde, falling in her face. He puts out a hand, infinitely gentle in spite of himself, pushes some of it back behind her ear, and sees that she is crying. She looks extraordinarily small and fragile, even less robust than he has anticipated. Without reflection, without reason, he picks her up, one arm under her knees, the other around her shoulders, and sits with her on his lap in the basket chair by the window. He rocks her gently and she continues to cry silently, soaking his shoulder inside his leather jacket, and he tells her, I'm here, I'm here, without any idea of what this might entail, for either of them. In this moment he knows that leaving her is impossible.

*

'She told me almost as soon as I arrived, within minutes. I can't remember what she said.'

Or she had tried. She had seemed to be upset about something specific, doubled up with embarrassment, and when asked what was the matter, had made a very cryptic beginning about looking for bath towels in her mother's room. It had emerged later that she had been putting them over her mattress at Lily and Vic's, and had got through several, stowing them in the dustbin because she didn't dare put them in the wash. He had put his arms around her and rocked her, saying into her hair that it didn't matter. At lunch Ilona had still been leaning against him. She had a lot of trouble eating, even then; she was overwrought. Lily had wanted her to go to bed after the meal but Daniel had guessed this was the worst suggestion. They had gone into town, just the two of them, and had talked of other things, Daniel striving to give her a space to make a more neutral beginning. In the city they had gone into one of the new bookshops with a café, where they had bought a few paperbacks together, E.Nesbit and Anne Fine, for her, Winnicott and R.D.Laing for him, or for both of them. They had sat reading bits in the café and she had had a hot chocolate. He had been aware that the prepared blankness had wholly vanished from his own eyes. After that, thoughts of abandonment really had begun to seem monstrous.

On the way back to Lily and Vic's he had gone into the pharmacy in the mall, leaving her to lurk in the baby section by the door while he went to buy what he needed, paracetamol, vitamins; he was beginning to feel like hell. When he came out, she had had time to slip a pale-blue dummy from a revolving rack into her inside pocket, unpaid for. When he discovered this item in France, much later, he knew without asking exactly when she had acquired it.

II

Four months previously.

Ilona wakes in the night. As the days go on, so the ritual of her going to bed diminishes. Hestia, exhausted by the effort of trying to appear normal, is becoming daily less able to pretend, and retires, practically unable to speak, as soon as the washing up is done, and then before. She sits at the kitchen table, her eyes hugely ringed, with a cup of tea, made by Ilona, which she sips, trying to control the shaking of her hands. Ilona, from coming unwillingly away from the television to help with the drying-up, has understood that it is for her to take the food out of the freezer, read the instructions, heat it, eat it, clear away. She has gone from doing this reluctantly to being extremely afraid. Hestia no longer scolds, no longer even asks her to tidy up, no longer mentions the mess, just drags herself up the stairs, concentrating, lies down on her stomach, goes under. In Ilona's room, the curtains go undrawn, t-shirts, unironed and unfolded, straggle on the chair and on the floor, looking grubby even when they are not; the sheets go unchanged.

Ilona wakes in the night, with wetness spreading under her. She calls, but Hestia, who cannot hear, does not come. Still in her damply clinging pyjamas, Ilona creeps into her mother's room, opens her lips almost soundlessly – 'Mamma' – , runs her fingertips over Hestia's cheek. Hestia sleeps on, lying strangely, slightly twisted, breathing very deeply. Her cheek feels oddly cool. Ilona goes back to her room, frozen inside, numb, unpeels her pyjama bottoms, pulls the sheet off her bed, and throws both into the bathroom. Then she curls herself tightly on the mattress-cover, and pulls the quilt up over her head.

'Hetty dear.' It is Lily. 'Hetty, are you alright?'

Ilona has come into Lily and Vic's garden on a Saturday morning, while Lily is seeing to the compost heap, kicked the watering can, and said, 'Mamma's dying.'

'You don't die from the flu, dear,' says Lily. 'Not these days. It was different when I was your age. Now you've got penicillin, central heating...'

Ilona loses no time, turns on her heel, lets herself in by the back door, goes to find Vic in his study, delivers the same message.

Vic comes out with her down the crazy-paving path, frowning, and Lily, seeing him come, stops her rake in mid-air. 'I think we'd better go round and see Hetty,' he says.

Hestia, amongst the ruins of the upstairs of the house, is slumped in a cane chair she looks as if she may never get out of. She is perspiring, her hair is damp and frizzy, her breath is short, her eyes sunken. The doctor is called, the house put to rights, Lily installs herself as sick-nurse. Hestia does not die that day, or even that week; she appears to get a little better and finds in due course the strength to get on the phone and to make arrangements to go to Vancouver to see her lawyer.

*

At Lily and Vic's, waiting for Daniel to rescue her, Ilona still wakes to the conscience of the same warm tide spreading over the rough cotton towel beneath her, not shameful, but insistently present, simply. Afterwards her skin, the insides of her thighs, are wet with a straightforward wetness. Quite silently in the bathroom she has learnt to sponge and dry, bundling the bathsheet into a plastic carrier bag, damp patch inwards, to be hidden under her bed and thrown away in the morning. She soothes herself back to sleep, thinking of Hestia stroking her hair, pretending to believe in Mamma, still here. She does not know yet how to formulate the things that evade her in her dreams.

*

And now, 'Alright, sweetheart?'

It is the end, for Ilona, of the first long day with Daniel, and the endearment already seems natural. He came not wanting her, but she seems to have marked herself out as his own. It is he she has leant against in the kitchen as they drink tea with Lily after the trip into town, silently asking for his arms to go round her, it is he who

23

takes her up to bed. Lily, allowing, she says, for jet lag and fatigue, has planned a big meal for the following night; the first day the three of them eat early in the kitchen before Victor gets home. Daniel and Ilona watch a TV comedy show too grown-up for her and then he tells her it's time for bed, picks her up in a fireman's lift and takes her upstairs.

*

Except that none of it was like that, the first meeting of Ilona and Daniel. Our Ilona is not in fact so clean, so clear, so easily endearing, nor so streamlined and co-ordinated with the décor of mature male existence; she is not versed in the ways of the world; she is, after all, ten years old. A glimpse, unawares: Daniel catches sight of her, alone, lolling on Lily and Vic's vast and unyielding black mock-leather sofa, not relaxed but broken, limbs all anyhow like an old jointed puppet with the elastic gone, her fluffy pale-blue jumper slightly grubby, the nape of her neck above it not entirely clean, one hand arrested in brushing across her face as if she had thought about putting her thumb in her mouth but proved somehow unequal to the task, the other squeezed against her pubis, anxiously, as if she were a much smaller child caught in a social dilemma in the incomprehensible adult world, a three-year-old who wants her mother. She is repellent in her hopeless grubbiness, and moving. He feels his soul wrap round her, in that moment, like a womb.

At this point he doesn't know whether it is for him to look after her or not, to offer comfort, a drink, a biscuit, so he tries this timorously, experimentally, to no response. She fails even to look at him, and it is at this moment that he realises that it is indeed for him to take her in hand, to save her from the barren spaces of Lily's unwieldy furniture. So he does in fact pick her up, takes her upstairs, sponges her face and neck, and as she doesn't object to this, goes the whole hog, gives her a bath, washes her hair. Poor Ilona, newly clean and comfortable and sleepy indeed, doesn't have the strength to protest.

There is something, nonetheless, in her reluctance to go up, her discomfiture at bedtime, the way she seems to want to tell him something but does not, that lets him know.

24

He sits on a corner of Lily's pale-green candlewick bedspread while Ilona cleans her teeth, wondering what to do now, what to say to her. One more to add to the list of adjectives in his head for this displaced and dysfunctional child: orphaned, weeping, miserable, and now nocturnally enuretic. Or so it would seem. He has no idea how to broach this subject with her, and just at this moment he doesn't see why it should be he who does.

She appears in his doorway, draped in a faded red nightshirt much too big for her, which must be Hestia's, stands with one hand still on the doorknob, and says, almost formally, 'Goodnight'.

'Come here.'

He holds his hands out to her, a gesture which in the bare three days of their acquaintance has not failed to work, but now she stands there, shamefaced, still clinging to the door. So now, he thinks, something will have to be said; her whole attitude acknowledges unease. But when he follows her down to Lily's boxroom to see her into bed it is no easier. He makes an attempt to sit her on his lap, but she almost lunges under the quilt in an effort to avoid this. Her face is closed, the subject impossible to broach. He reads to her, *The Story of the Amulet*, in which children transplant themselves at will, in a decorous Georgian manner, in time and space, and she is quiet; he is pretty sure she is only pretending to be asleep. He pats her shoulder, awkwardly, and withdraws. Here, then, is what she was trying to tell him from the first.

Next day, after Vic has left for work, and Lily, sometime later, for her voluntary service at a rehab centre, leaving behind a stale smell of substantial breakfasts eaten at a leisurely pace which they both find depressing, and which they have chased away by tacit consent, opening windows, and scaling down also the slightly nauseating array on the table to manageable proportions – fruit juice, cracottes, yoghurts – Daniel finds himself liking her rather better. The sun slants through Lily's spotless panes onto Ilona's pale hair; she has put on a bell-shaped cream jumper, wider at the bottom than at the top and somehow angelic, and looks pretty in it, a pretty little girl, not the disturbing overgrown toddler he had thought to glimpse the previous evening. But the expression on her face, he notes, is perpetually uncertain.

Nonetheless, they develop a sort of synchronicity, in spite of his reluctance; it is he and she versus Lily and Vic. Not that he has anything against them – these immensely kind people with whose lives Hestia must, after all, have become enmeshed somewhere along the way. But there is something in him which holds out instinctively against so much chintz and floor polish, against the sterile deserts of the immense synthetic sofas in the lounge, the candlewick and the bedside shades in matching pastel shades upstairs; and, above all and in spite of himself, at the thought of Ilona amongst all this, like nobody's raggedy abandoned doll, breaking the clean day-time lines of the furniture, with Lily aching to tidy her up and put her away.

Now Ilona sits and fiddles with her yoghurt rather than eating it, and she says at last, without looking at him, that there is something she has to tell him. He takes her spoon out of her hand and lays it down, draws her to him and stands her between his knees with her back to him, his arms around her waist, and this time he is wholehearted, none of him is acting. However apparently willingly he had leapt to read to her in bed, take her for walks, sit with her, in the first couple of days, it had not been quite substantial, but a day or two have brought the realisation that he is real to her, and indispensable, that she counts on him absolutely. And that now he has stopped acting with her, she will, he knows as a certainty, allow herself to be real with him.

But she doesn't know where to start, and makes a little inarticulate noise, and he pulls her up onto his knee, properly.

'I think,' he tells her, not listening to himself talking to her for the first time since they met, 'it might have something to do with this area' – he gives her bottom a vague pat – 'at night? Hm?'

She buries her face in his shoulder, not crying, or not yet, but he can feel her heart racing, and guesses she must be blushing her deep crimson blush.

'How long have you – how long has this been happening, sweetheart?'

She sniffs and says, half-reluctant, half-relieved, 'A long time. But more – since Mamma – '

'I know.' He is trying to know.

'I need you to buy me something', she says into his shoulder, barely audible.

'That's ok.' Buy her something? Are they still on the same track? But she can't get it out. In the end she slithers off his knee and leads him up to her room, where she roots around in a holdall stuffed under her bed and finally produces, without looking at him, an empty blue plastic packet, which she has folded up very small, and which he opens out to reveal a picture of a sleeping child and a label: absorbent pants, ten pairs. She watches him take this in – later it seems to him that his idiotic slowness in understanding that now she was actually telling him, now she wanted to reveal, not to hide, must have made it harder for her. But this time it is she who climbs onto his lap and burrows into him, moulding him around her, modelling his flesh to exactly accommodate her shape. And not only his flesh, he later thinks, but all his being.

So much manoeuvring, he reflects, becomes necessary for the simplest thing when you are ten years old and without money or any means of living your life discreetly. They go to the hypermarket she indicates, and pick up a few items of clothing for him – he packed so little – and some groceries, and a pack of peach-coloured underwear with little butterflies on it for her, and just slip in the awkward package, face down in the trolley with the grey t-shirt Ilona has picked out for him draped over them, as if it was something they had had to get for some neighbour child, for somebody having no connection at all with Ilona, who pointedly studies the adverts on the pinboard while Daniel puts their purchases through the checkout.

It is only later, seeing her into bed that night, that he mentions that he could go and find a mattress-cover from next door and bring her own sheets over, and they are, after all, washable. But when Ilona says, emphatically, no, not in Lily's house, he understands. She turns slowly, and looks up into his eyes, as if taking an exact reading of the extent to which she can trust him. How right she is, Daniel thinks, but he smiles and looks back, guiltily attempting limpidity.

'You won't tell Lily, will you?' She is suddenly wide awake and sitting up, after what he had thought was the completion of the bedtime ceremony.

'Of course I won't tell Lily.'

'Or Vic.'

'Or Vic.'

He pushes her gently back down and she accepts this gesture, curls back up and sighs, but reaches for his hand, detaining him still. Her eyes are about to close when he remembers the bear which he has not yet thought to give her. He brings it in and tucks it under the quilt. 'You just come and call me if you have a bad dream,' he says. 'Ok? Just come into my room and wake me up. Don't worry about it at all.'

He stays with her, talking her into sleep in an almost-whisper, until she lets his hand go, and a little beyond.

Later, when Ilona does wake, as usual a few seconds too late, and Daniel, who has heard her cry out in her dreams, has come in without needing to be called, kindly and matter-of-fact in spite of persistent jet lag, she has an uncomfortable sense, even in the face of this unjudging tenderness, of having given herself too easily away. As if she couldn't hold anything in, she indistinctly formulates; as if she had to give everything away. Worse, she is not sure that this is entirely covered by the fact that she has been caught in the babyish act of wetting her sheets. Vulnerability is a word which has not yet entered her vocabulary, but when it does, in memory she will recognise it, here.

*

'Papa. Papa.'

'Ilona... you know that I'm not actually – I'm not your father...'

'I don't want you to be my father. I haven't got a father. You're my *papa*.'

III

There is the funeral, to which Ilona refuses to go. The vicar, who says he understands this perfectly, arranges a brief ceremony in a side-chapel of the Anglican church in which Hestia is to be buried. Ilona, who when asked has expressed a wish that the coffin be covered, lays on it at the vicar's suggestion ten single pale roses, criss-crossing its length, to signify the years of their lives together, mother and child. He then asks her to light a thick plain candle which will burn all night in a surround of cool marble, to represent the mother's love in the child, which will never die. Daniel appreciates this reversal of surround and surrounded, the enwombed becoming the enwombing. A perpetuation of life itself, he thinks, suggestive of Ilona's own carrying of children, although this is probably more than the vicar intended. The vicar prays neatly and succinctly, in perhaps anxiously premeditated phrases, for Ilona's life with Daniel, and then Daniel takes his ward back to Lily and Vic's for a slightly grotesque semblance of a family supper. Very little is eaten at all, and none by Ilona, whom at this moment Daniel doesn't dare to coax. She doesn't cry when he takes her up to bed, but seems peculiarly distant and reticent, this child who climbed onto his lap almost from the first and let him offer his then-treacherous comfort and caresses. Daniel sits on the edge of her bed, stroking her hair, which she allows; the build-up of weeks of insomnia and the shock of the loss have combined to make her at least fall easily into sleep, although her nights are punctured and uneasy.

The ceremony proper is the following day. Daniel and Vic go off dark-suited in the car, while Lily, who feels unable to leave Ilona, keeps her busy in the kitchen, cutting the crusts off small sandwiches and arranging them on disposable catering platters, plastic silver and cardboard gold. There is a play by Noel Coward on the radio, to which Ilona apparently listens intently; euphonious voices confidently calling in a country house on an island she has never seen.

By the time the party arrives back at the house, several of the guests have dropped back home to collect their daughters, Ilona's classmates from her French convent-school, who come in and greet her and then stand embarrassed around the foot of the stairs, oddly grown-up in their discomfiture. Emmanuelle, Lore, Justine, Pauline, Célia, Chloë. They have decided, in a body, to come in black, and the effect is anachronistic, disturbing, like servant-girls cast in a period drama, thinks Daniel. Ilona, from the second stair, dressed in a navy velvet frock and patent shoes and once more stroking the cat, feels their presence after a week's absence from school as unaccountably bizarre. They tell her about the final manifestation of the dance-sequence they performed at the parents' evening, in which Ilona would otherwise have taken part. She was replaced by Célia, who gallantly gave up her tennis training to make up the six. Chloë, awkward, a little large and not always liked, does not dance.

When the dance talk dies out, they drift into the conservatory where the buffet is set out, but do not approach the tables. Ilona sits in a huge wing chair and adults come up to her, make kindly, allusive attempts at valedictory remarks, and move away. It is Daniel who eventually sees that she sits too still, too steadfast; the cat, once more discouraged, has deserted her lap. He gathers her up and takes her upstairs, laying her on her bed, and reads to her, about Polly and Digory, an old-fashioned little boy and girl in far-off unimaginable London, who by means of being tricked into donning magic rings, are transported into different worlds. If in a mistaken attic on a holiday afternoon you take a mysteriously humming yellow ring from a tray and put it on, you are whirled instantaneously to another dimension, the Wood between the Worlds, where there are any number of possible pools, channels to other spheres of time and space. The children work out that the magic substance in the yellow rings wants to get back to its place of origin, while the green rings, which Digory's great uncle has thoughtfully, albeit uncertainly, provided against their return, are repulsed by their place of origin, and may thus propel you back into your own world, or, equally, into another. Ilona likes this story and knows it well, or at least the beginning of it, and thrills when Polly is dispatched, destination unknown, without a green ring, not even a chance of a return ticket. Daniel remembers reading it to her on his visit when she was six: she had asked what would happen if the children were to put on both rings at the same time, and Daniel had said that probably the effects would neutralise each other and they would stay in the same place.

Reminded, now, of this, she stills like an animal unsure of the intention of a caress, and decides finally on a question which allows only one response, sounding like the six-year-old he remembers: 'Will I like it in France?'

Daniel and Ilona go one afternoon in their last few days in Canada to look at Hestia's grave. She has been buried on a slope, overlooking the sea. The day is unseasonably cold. Ilona, in a woolly hat and gloves, stands at her mother's graveside uncertain what to do, when they have laid the flowers: extravagantly forced lilies, chosen by Ilona, which Daniel knows will blacken and freeze. The headstone has not yet been erected. He asks if she would like him to leave her alone, and she shakes her head. After a little they make their way down a narrow cliff path to the beach, and once at the bottom Ilona, with no warning, begins to run on the hard wet sand, down towards the sea and continuing along the shoreline, fast, almost galloping, until her strength gives out, when she subsides onto a rock, her white bobble-hat bright against the heavy sky and sea. Daniel takes his time catching up. He meets her wordlessly and without touching, leaning one foot on the rock beside her, until eventually she says, 'Shall we go?'

'Shall we take another look?'

Ilona shakes her head without looking at him. He swings her up onto one hip, like a much smaller child, and carries her back towards the car. After a few miles, driven in silence, she suddenly bursts into tears and tells Daniel desperately that she has to go back, he must take her back; she is crying hysterically. As soon as he can, Daniel pulls into a lay-by, stops the car, and tells her that of course he'll take her back, she only has to say. He pulls her onto his knee, bumping her awkwardly against the steering-wheel, and tries for a long moment to rock, to soothe. Once quiet, Ilona says that she doesn't want to go back after all. Daniel says they can sit and think about it for a little, unhurried, and puts the radio on, still holding her against him, her face buried in his chest, inside his jacket. They wait like that for some time, but she doesn't change her mind. She finally wriggles back into the passenger seat, where after a few minutes she goes to sleep, not waking till they get back to Lily's over an hour later.

*

31

Days are spent packing and sorting in the house next door. It is felt that nothing should be arranged over Ilona's head, that she should be aware of the distribution of furniture, mostly to Lily and Vic or into store, should decide which of her things should be sent on in due course to Nice, what she needs more immediately, what she can't from the first do without. Labels are made out, smaller items are regrouped, but they have agreed that the house will not be packed up and emptied until Ilona has left with Daniel, to spare her feelings. Nevertheless, she cries when Lily says that her last year's summer things will be too small by the spring and are not worth sending; Daniel says to pack them anyway. Even these preliminaries upset her; she will not believe that things will not be allowed to disappear, and follows Daniel around, trailing from room to room: 'Can I have my puzzles in Nice? What's happening to the chicken egg-cups? Are we taking Mamma's goosefeather quilt? I want *all* my books...' Each request is designed to be less easy to meet than the last, more likely to be denied. She is anxious and mistrustful, picking her way with him in a way she hasn't yet done, narrowly close in her anxiety to whining. Lily, seeing this and that Daniel is preoccupied with envisaging the practical arrangements, sets her to cutting pieces of sellotape for the labels and lining them up along the edge of a shelf.

It is during the last look-round before departure that she climbs onto a high stool and pockets a pair of dice, feeling that they are certain to be overlooked; too small to be labelled or packed or even noticed. Yet she has noticed them and fiddled with them periodically for years, since she has been tall enough to reach the shelf, on which, when she was small, little dangerous objects were put purposely out of her way. She has always put them back. Now she takes them secretly, with a feeling of obscure satisfaction.

Ilona slips the dice into an inside pocket of the shoulder bag she has acquired as part of the trousseau Lily has been putting together day by day since the news of Hestia's death, for going away. Ilona has never owned a bag before apart from her school satchel and a fluorescent PVC knapsack, for her swimming things. The new bag is made of soft wide-channelled corduroy and is black; put down, it gives the impression of some curled-up furry creature, a familiar. In the lining are a variety of pockets for her supposed make-up, keys, credit cards, passport and so on. Of these she only possesses the last, so there are available spaces to fill up. Thus she legitimises the presence of the dice.

*

Ilona has an idea of France, which consists essentially of the Eiffel Tower against a lurid sunset. It is the perceived glamour of this destination which helpfully serves to make their departure, next day, exciting for her, and leaving less appalling. She refers to Lily's gift as her flight bag, and in it she has Daniel's bear, which, she says, she will allow to look out of the window so that he knows he is going all the way back to France.

In the dusk, a draining time for departures, it is Lily who cracks as they disappear into the departure lounge. Just out of sight of Ilona, who has been turning round and waving till the last, although Daniel has not wanted to make too much of the fact that once you are through, you cannot go back – the sort of rule, he remembers, with pain and exasperation, that Hestia was very good at confounding – Lily buries her head in Victor's shoulder and weeps, blindly.

Going through the safety checks, the signal begins to bleep for Ilona. She is told to take off her watch and bracelet and earrings, and she hands them to Daniel who is already through. The bleep continues and the official takes her bag, which contains ostensibly only two books, the teddy-bear from Daniel, and a few toiletries Lily has thought necessary for her journey. Ilona digs out the dice reluctantly, and they are put through the machine in a little plastic box. Inside the smaller of the two, the red one, a bead of metal shows up clearly on the screen, lodged to one side: it is apparently a weighted die. The officials joke about Ilona being too young to gamble, and let her through.

After the excitement of take-off, Ilona is overtaken with melancholy. In the window-seat, she sits with Daniel's arm protectively around her as if she might fall out, the armrest between their two seats raised, looking down at the beauty of the evening sky while it is still to be made out. Holding her face away from him, her body nonetheless leans in; his arm pulls her towards him at the waist. He feels, then, he is later to believe, the moment when she sinks into her doom, when the waters close over her head and something inside her registers one degree below tolerable. She doesn't cry, but across the screen of her mind is stamped, unknown to Daniel, the phrase, Too cold for snow. He sits and strokes her hair while she continues to turn her back and then when the drinks trolley begins its discreet rattle suggests a book. Obedient, Ilona brings her bag out from under her seat and produces one of the oddly eclectic selections peculiar to her age, *Jennings* and *David Copperfield* . Daniel knows that the former will make her giggle but takes the Dickens, for its oblique commentary, he thinks, on the moment: *So I lost her. So I saw her afterwards, in my sleep at school – a silent presence near my bed – looking at me with the same intent face – holding up her baby in her arms...* Ilona brings out Daniel's bear too and sits it in the crook of her arm. Daniel's newly acute observation of ten-year-old girls has registered that though they often have furry bears and toys about them, these are usually very small, clipped to a jacket or the strap of a schoolbag. Ilona does not hide hers, although it sits eight inches high.

As she continues to listen, Daniel continues to read, with interruptions for drinks and meals, which Ilona barely touches. The man in the seat next to Daniel, middle-aged, apparently benign, perhaps an academic, when asked if he is disturbed by this *lecture*, claims that he is delighted to overhear and begs him not to stop. When Ilona finally allows herself to be wrapped in a cellular blanket, to lean back and close her eyes, Daniel explains to this man that she has lost her mother. This will become, over and over, his phrase of introduction, of explanation, and it is almost always initially misunderstood. To follow the announcement of her mother's death with the denial of his own paternity would seem unnecessarily callous within Ilona's hearing. It is not only this. It is perhaps also that he still finds his own part in the proceedings as ludicrously unlikely as it must seem from the outside.

Daniel does not ask about the dice – he isn't yet very regular about asking – but in the plane, bored at last by *David Copperfield*, Ilona brings them out and starts to fiddle with them. In the end they devise a game, which consists of the exchange of stories: for a score of six a story must be told about when the thrower was six, and so on. The other is quite at liberty to ask questions.

34

The game becomes a sort of *I Spy* into the soul. Sometimes stories succeed each other with several quick throws of the dice, sometimes just one shake will produce a topic which will outlast the plane journey and go on intermittently for days or longer. So it is that each spins the fine thread of their past for the other, so it is that they gather fragile substance and come into being.

There is no rule about finishing one story before going onto the next. Neither are the dice any guarantor of truth or even of truth telling. Sometimes Ilona, experimentally, will lie, throwing smoke screens, telling him something which seems to have some other story or circumstance behind it, wanting to be asked but unable to tell. She wants him to provide the parts she can't remember, and he tells her stories they both know are made up, but which fill in the gaps nonetheless, and in doing so help to bind her to him. Daniel, who wasn't there, tells Ilona about when she was two. She tells, and doesn't tell, about the first birthday party she remembers clearly, at four, fireworks in the garden, a sparkler and the magic of drawing daisy loops on the sky, a pure and enraptured happiness, possibly never to be known again.

The principle is very simple, but the game, like the red die, is weighted. It is possible that Daniel knows or remembers more about Ilona when she was three, four, five or six than she does herself, and age nine for her is the recent past whereas for him it is part of a cloud of childhood, virtually undifferentiated in comparison to the vivid immediacy of her own. The sum of the dice will always span Ilona's entire existence and more, for she is not yet eleven and twelve is still unimaginably far away, whereas their total leaves thirty years of Daniel's life unaccounted for. So for Ilona they add the scores of the two dice together, for Daniel, when he exhausts his childhood, they multiply instead of adding, and almost reach the peak: six sixes, thirty-six. The five remaining years of his life are compensation, more or less in proportion, for Ilona's missing one and a half when she throws two sixes. This period offers, in the event, limitless opportunity, at least for her, for speculation. But the game is also one of requests for reassurance, as the weighted die turns into a crystal ball. What is going to happen, she endlessly and impossibly asks, when she is eleven, twelve, and will she like it? Daniel, cheating, offers concrete information in response, describing the house at Ste-Marie and the flat in Nice, avoiding, as she does, any mention of school.

The game with the dice is also a safeguard: their habit is to throw both together, so the lowest possible score is two, for the moment further back cannot be reached, is not accessible. He knows what Hestia has told Ilona about the circumstances of her conception and birth, which were bleak and violent, for this is the sort of information with which she has been prodigal in her endless letters, but this will not prevent Ilona from asking more questions, later on, when Daniel will cease to be for her a miraculous being, incarnation of a fantasy, magically air-dropped into her life, and then she will start to tessellate the pieces of her past, finding them perhaps mismatched and after all unaccountable.

The game acquires its own numerology. For Ilona, twelve is the magic number; beyond it seems to be outside the reach of her imagination, or even, perhaps, her interest. She asks Daniel what happened to him when he was twelve, and he extemporises, even prevaricates: a holiday in Switzerland, a puppy, roller skates, supposing that these things must have happened somewhere along the line. Later a vision of being twelve comes back to him, unlooked for. He is on a train, going home, thank God, from boarding school, but not for long; it must be half term or an exeat. It is cold outside and already almost dark, it must be the autumn of his first term away. Ever present in his mind is the appalling and ineffaceable memory of his daily tears at the breakfast table when mail from home is distributed and his mother's words speak to him in her voice – source of a shame so bitter and so deep that sometimes he would rather be dead than face it. These tears are not the only vice for which he is taunted; there is also religion, and a nascent moral earnestness he can trace but not disguise. Daily life has become a question of trying, more or less successfully, to keep out of the way of harm, to deflect conflict, to avoid finding himself on his own where he can be got at. Now, in the dingy compartment train, he is already mentally in his mother's dimly lit dining room with his back to the piano, drinking soup as she sits beside him, bravely catching up on the pathetically superficial details he will certainly offer about his painfully-borne absence – who won at soccer, whether he is likely to beat Miller to the end-of-term prize – smiling above the tears in her eyes. But there is a trick, a trap, which he is not prepared for: the first thing his father asks him for in the car at the station is his report card, to which Daniel has given no thought and which he is not aware of having in his possession. And unbelievably, he is not allowed to get into the car, in which his father has already stowed his bag, but is immediately sent back on the next train, to fetch the report – and failing that, his father requires, a note from his housemaster explaining the reason why. His mother remonstrates: there is a phone box on the station, all he has to do is telephone and it will be put in the post, to arrive no doubt next day or the day after. To no avail. So off he goes again to the hated place, arriving to his housemaster's puzzlement in the middle of the family supper, causing disturbance and embarrassment; the card, which was to have gone out next day, has to be found and copied; dinner, on the table, gets cold; Matron interrupts her own supper and drives the miserable boy back to the station. At the school, there are no reproaches, only bewilderment and unease, which are somehow harder to bear.

The report, when it is read, is not much good, and Daniel is given a hasty, silent meal and sent to bed.

For Daniel, the game with the dice becomes a sort of bizarre multiplication table, suggestive of a surreal and disturbing logic. Three times the treachery of his father equals the day, or almost, he found David dead. For just as for Ilona the game stalls at twelve, signifying bounds she has not yet reached, so for Daniel, thirty-six marks what once seemed the end of the charted territory of his existence: the logical end of the upward curve marked by growing up, the getting of an education, the making of a career, a home, of turning an existence into a life, a life with David always there, the anchor weighing him down, the bay to come back to, and the person in whom he had found at last a true reflection of himself, acceptable to both of them. Although this, once true, was beginning, even at that time, to seem less so. What bound them was becoming less solid. And not even 'at that time.' It was precisely because of the shifting ground on which, after years, they had found themselves carping and fighting and sulking, that David had decided to take a sabbatical, to go away, alone, to think. To think over whether he wanted Daniel to continue to figure in his existence.

David had been murdered. For what had seemed like a very long time, Daniel had not heard from him at all, had not expected to. This was part of the punishment, the preparation before being got rid of, the toughening up. He, for his part, had affected a carapace, taking over the empty space David's absence left in the Waterloo flat, to which they had moved after Balham, beginning first to overflow into and then to live in the deserted space and periodically to invite others to join him there. They both had their mobile phones, should an emergency arise.

In the event the emergency, when it had arisen, had left David no time to reach for his phone. Daniel remembers, and will always remember, hearing while he lay half-reading in bed, late at night, not long before or not long after the shipping forecast, an item on the news: a British man has been found dead in Thailand. The body has not yet been identified. This had set off alarm bells, but not loudly enough. He had assumed that David, hearing about this, would soon now be in touch, to reassure.

David had been murdered for the sake of the contents of his rucksack. His assassin had later apologised, and the King of Thailand had sent a personal message of sympathy. The first, unrecognised announcement had become in retrospect much the most sinister.

IV

Neither Ilona nor Daniel was aware that the dice had been stolen, or acquired, by Hestia, from the house in Balham. There were two of them, mismatched in size and colour: one made of cream bakelite, stamped with large, slightly misplaced, black dots, looked as if it had once been part of a children's game, the other, smaller and heavier, the one which turned out to be weighted, was dark red.

An abundance of objects, of clutter, peacefully resided in the Balham house, belonging really to no-one, or to no-one living, not much cherished and not much missed in its constituent pieces, but giving the house, in its entirety, a comforting lining, the soft dense habitation of years, the dark brown-red shredded comfort of the womb. There were of course books, no doubt thousands of them, and small pieces of sculpture, deliberately collected and pictures, photographs and postcards written and unwritten, but strewn among all this, a complex and inextricable trail, was a whole miscellany, sometimes fascinating, sometimes, to Hestia, threatening, of small objects: dolls dressed and undressed, a cardboard fashion-dressing book, showing a very young Lady Diana with multiple outfits, leaning against the bottom corner of a vast greenish-mottled mirror; a plastic hairband from the seventies, decorated with huge multi-coloured flowers, one of which was missing; a forties handbag in brown patent leather, an odd high-heeled red sandal; was it to femininity or to something else that these objects paid tribute? There was irony here, but she was not sure at whom or what it was directed. Shared by Daniel and David and another couple, it was a house, not just of men, but where women had no function, no purpose – or it was a purpose which escaped Hestia. Once, over from France and staying in the house for the weekend of a friend's wedding, she had brought down a Laura Ashley dress to iron, a simple silk shift, yet long, yet luxuriant, yet feminine in a way that the fashion write-ups describe as 'delicious' – and there had been exclamations of delight, of enthusiasm, the translucent fabric had been touched, weighed up, examined with care; what had disconcerted her at the time had been that this celebration of the dress was directed so very much at the garment itself, and not at all at her, standing ironing in her underwear, a bathrobe hanging open from her shoulders: here's the real thing, she had wanted to say, I've even got the curves to wear it.

But in the Balham house femininity could only be received through masculinity, the men not being receptive to it in its pure state. All of them would kiss her on the lips for hello and goodnight, not because she was a woman but because the man-to-woman social kiss was something they had appropriated, between gay men. When they kissed her like that, it was a double bluff: what she got was not a man-to-woman social kiss, but a secondary inversion of this, because the norm for them was man-to-man.

Once it had been with pain that she had recognised, one night when she had had come back late to find them all reclining on the floor of the summer-house, that their camped-up admiration of her, their touches, their caresses, their suggestions, owed nothing to herself but were the product of the drugs she later realised they had been taking. She knew why they took them, or partly why, and Hestia, whose first fumblings with a boy from church had been interrupted by the cry, 'That's fornication!', had to arrange with herself not to think about it. To keep the knowledge somewhere safe and sealed.

The dice, however, had been among that part of the paraphernalia which could be classed as neutral, the accumulated clutter of every household. They had been discovered on that same wedding weekend, in a search for a last-minute safety pin, lying at the bottom of an ancient cracked marmalade pot, hidden between layers of cards and bric-a-brac on a long gracious mantelpiece. The marmalade pot, in glazed white ceramic, with violet and sage-green flowers and a horseshoe-shaped hole in the lid for the spoon, proved to contain several small gold safety pins, a few dusty rubber bands, an old nappy pin with rusting hasp and dangerously bent shaft, a length of ancient black velvet ribbon, a foil figure seven from a birthday cake, an odd earring like a Christmas bauble, a rusty needle with its point thrust into a screw of paper, and the dice. Hestia had taken the pot upstairs, in case some other vital item could be conjured from its innards, and had left it on the shelf behind the bed in the spare room, which had become its new home, for there it had stayed, for years, until she spent her last night in that room, the night of the conception of Ilona. The life of the house was made up of these silent transfers, these minute upheavals.

The marmalade pot had been a distraction, on the last night she had ever stayed in Balham, its contents somehow comforting, its quiet and unformulated mystery: who had put these things here, and when; if the search for one gold pin could bear witness to a whole wedding, to what little feasts and rites of passage did these other objects belong? She had thought of the unknown birthday cake – seven or twenty-seven or seventy-seven? Whose child, whose lover or grandparent? From where had they made the journey to the house, where were they now, did they even remember? She thought of the Balham house, passing into endless existences – and out. The house went on collecting a little part of all those who came there.

The dice were contained in the ribbon, which had accommodated itself to the circumference of the pot, and fell in a soft spiral. She worked them gently up the cracked ceramic side, mended with a trail of uneven beads of yellowish glue, and sat that night playing with them, idly waiting for a double six to fall on the bedside table. The activity was soothing because it helped to avoid thinking of other things. She couldn't guess at the beginning of Ilona's tenuous formulation within her, but later she wondered if she had been playing a game of chance, and if so, what the stakes were. Perhaps it should have been a coin she played with: Ilona or no Ilona. Heads you win, tails you lose.

The microscopic heads and tails were already at work inside her, swimming blindly in the febrile race to exist. Hestia, who had been periodically tortured by existence and the vacillation of her will to exist, had always wanted to be able to reverse that process, to shrink back through womanhood to adolescence through quick slim pubescence, past dull childhood and back to the womb; she had willed her own disintegration into nothingness, the reversal of the sperm; turn back, oh, turn back, swim the other way. Her dearest and most impossible wish: not to exist. To exit from one's own life once in it is simply to take a short-cut to the end, to conform to the cycle, and does not constitute an escape. What she wanted was to turn back time. What she wanted was never to have been at all.

She inserted the dice through the open inch of the zip of her handbag, hearing them fall into the clutter at the bottom, for her journey, she thought, although it was not yet clear where she would or could go. But she might need them. To help her decide.

Through the years in Canada, the dice had stayed in Hestia's bedroom, a sort of testament to chance, as the daily miracle of Ilona's presence, Ilona's existence, unfolded. Motherhood became the whole of Hestia's affective life, she felt not just love for her daughter but a fusion with her; their existence was shared, they were a part of one another. There was to be none of the alienation, for Ilona, of battling, an ill-prepared child-warrior, in an incomprehensible adult world. She was constantly held, kissed, caressed, listened to, shown, played with, actively cherished, loved.

The dice in Hestia's house were out of their context. Hers was a house that held little clutter. Although she had managed in time to settle into domestic and daily existence, to cry to the impulse which had whispered slyly for so long, If you don't need it, throw it out, don't buy that, it'll mean one thing more to move, Oh reason not the need! – she still had difficulty accumulating more than could be left without too much pain should the time come. But the dice sat on, on a highish shelf, approached only occasionally by Ilona's small exploratory fingers, which would displace them only temporarily, and which left them, anyway, mostly undisturbed. In a decade, they had barely moved.

V

Arrival in Paris: Ilona's eyes open to high-rise tower blocks and not the Eiffel Tower. Daniel has explained to her that they will be staying just one night, really just a few hours, in an airport hotel, that it will be better if they get to Ste-Marie as quickly as possible, to settle in, to recover from the journey, that they will have ample opportunity to spend time later in Paris, where his friends have flats in which they will be delighted for Ilona to stay. Obliged to make the best of this for the moment, Ilona has vowed inwardly to make Paris of the hotel, to enjoy it to the full. Daniel, who occasionally uses this hotel on business trips, has talked of a pool with a jacuzzi, and Ilona, who is naturally unworldly, is prepared to be impressed by this. But when the time comes, the fountains in the entrance-hall, the pastel-carpeted mirrored lifts, do not seem to make any impression at all. A sort of blankness seems to have settled over her. Daniel remembers, with guilt but also with incredulity – simultaneously at where he has got himself now and at how he could have contemplated such dastardly action – why he had chosen to stay in Paris: he had been planning to spend a few days reading in cafés, visiting galleries and perhaps making an investment or two, seeing friends, in brief, breathing an immense sigh of relief after a difficult coup pulled off: getting rid of the prospect of Ilona.

'Sleep?' he suggests, when she has inspected their room – a double bed alongside which a child's bed has been added (this seemed the only possible arrangement, she will not sleep in a strange place on her own) – and the gilt and white marble shower, which she notes, but does not comment on.

'No. Swimming.'

Daniel thinks that perhaps an interlude is a good idea, while they, so recently delivered from their lightning passage through the sky, get their bearings in time and space. Although the pool has been mentioned, neither they nor Lily have somehow thought to pack Ilona's swimsuit in the hand luggage, and the rest is being sent on directly to Nice. Daniel will get better at anticipating this sort of oversight, which just at the moment is inclined to make Ilona cry and to make him feel depressingly unparental. She does not yet know, as her mother found out, that much of life's necessary equipment can be bought in airports and at railway stations.

At reception they are directed to a glass-fronted shop in which they find a rail of swimming gear and a large stock of soft toys, many sporting the logos of airlines on miniature t-shirts. Asked if she would like one, Ilona says that she prefers the bear he has already given her. Daniel is both flattered and disappointed, feeling confusedly that he ought to give her something more. Guilt about the spirit in which the bear was purchased still gnaws; he is ashamed to see that she has become attached to it. But now she is pleased with her new swimsuit, in navy and white horizontal stripes, with a row of cherry red boats and anchors sailing jauntily across the chest.

Seeing her emerge after a few minutes from her cubicle and cross the poolside from the opposite end, Daniel is struck by the contrast between this cheerful swimwear and the pallor, almost the greyness, of Ilona's small face, the boniness of her hips and shoulders. They have swum together in Canada and she has not looked as stricken as this. As she enters the shallow water and begins to wade over to him, a little Indian boy throws an inflatable ball hopefully towards her. Ilona splashes past as if she hasn't even seen; perhaps she has not. The Indian child, small enough to feel real disappointment at this, abandons the ball angrily and turns away, while Daniel attempts to mime to the father, with his expression, I'm so sorry, she's lost her mother. Bringing out a version of this phrase, compulsively, when he finds himself crossing the Indian's path a few minutes later, he meets with the response, 'My son has lost his mother, too.' Their eyes meet, the Indian hoping perhaps to read in Daniel's' the reflection of his own unmanageable grief for his wife. Once again Daniel feels fraudulent.

In the morning, or their morning, which is already largely afternoon in France, Ilona is lethargic and monosyllabic. Daniel reminds her that they will be coming back to Paris, but this does not seem to be what is on her mind. Checking in late because both have had trouble waking up, they find themselves separated on the plane. In the hire car, which will be picked up that evening, she says very little but looks, Daniel observes, at the colours she has never seen, at the unexpected blues of the hills low on the horizon, and exclaims, once, at the expansive caress of the spring sun, brilliant even in the early evening. A narrow track leads down for almost a mile to the *mas* at St-Marie, ranked contours of vineyards spread over the plane, and, within view of the house stand the remains of a medieval castle on the low hillside opposite, within which, Daniel tells Ilona, the ghosts of espaliered trees can still be seen etched on the walls, where live wood and sap once ate into stone and dust.

Daniel supposes that he is inconsistent to expect exclamations of pleasure, of delight, when he has so recently resented the prospect of her arrival, but her silence can be read as condemnatory. Taking her inside, depositing her luggage, which seems suddenly absurdly little with which to transfer yourself from one side of the world to the other, Daniel feels strangely that the situation calls primarily for courtesy, settling in a house guest.

The room in which Ilona is to sleep is large and square, with hexagonal terracotta tiles on the floor and vine leaves framing the grilles at the windows, which are relatively small and high up, for the room is on the ground floor. There is a loosely woven purple Indian cover thrown over the large, low bed with a ladder-backed chair next to it, a blackened iron table pushed against the far wall, an empty armoire, in heavy, ancient wood. Next to the bed are three shallow steps, leading up to a door which gives onto the room which is Daniel's when he is here. Ilona's room holds no trace at all of her expected arrival, as Daniel had not intended to bring her home.

Ilona seems far away, beyond speech. Daniel suggests something to eat and she allows herself to be led into the kitchen, where she sits stiffly at the table, looking at nothing, refusing to look. It is apparent that she cannot and will not eat.

'Catch up on a bit of sleep?' says Daniel. There is no reply but she follows him back to her room. He shows her how to operate her shower, brings out towels, finds her soap and shampoo, opens the smallest of her cases, in which a few changes of clothes have been put to be easily accessible on arrival. 'No,' says Ilona when he starts to lay these on the bed. Daniel, not entirely oblivious to the psychology of unpacking, puts the case back on the floor. And then, he is later to tell Dr. Echs, 'I should have undressed her myself, bathed her, put her into bed and stayed with her until she went to sleep; I should have let her cry, I should have – '

Dr. Echs asks why he did not.

'She seemed not to want me to be there', says Daniel. 'I was trying to give her time to settle in in her own way.'

Alone, Daniel eats and lingers over the paper, makes coffee, sits on the *terrasse*, closes his eyes and thinks about the unlikelihood of the last two weeks ever having happened at all. The pastel sky gives way imperceptibly to a velvety, scented darkness. After some time, he treads softly down the hall to Ilona's room. The moon shines through the window: the room is just as he left it, and she isn't there.

Less than five minutes after the onset of panic, Daniel is in his car driving down the track to get onto the main road and then the *route nationale*, while Antoine, the farming tenant and neighbour, checks the other way. Daniel is sweating, his heart racing, but he manages to drive slowly, checking each side of the road: what if she has been injured, abducted even? One hears of such things, of sleepovers in innocent family gardens, waking up with one child less. And if she has gone off, willingly, how could he have been so stupid, so blind, as to have let it happen?

In the end – after barely twenty minutes – Daniel catches sight of her easily enough, in the almost-dark, because she is wearing pale jeans, still the ones she'd had on on the plane. He veers the car into the lay-by, too fast, aggressive in his haste, and jumps out. Ilona screams and flings an arm over her face, dodging backwards; dazzled by the headlights, she hasn't had time to recognise him, or the car, which is not the one he has driven from the airport. He pulls her forward and into the passenger seat, where she sits, shaking, breathing hard, not crying. He asks her if she is alright and she does not, perhaps cannot, respond. As they pull out he has an unpleasant sensation of eyes, watching, from the lorries parked for the night.

After the tortuous outward journey, they are back at the *mas* within minutes. But when the engine stops Ilona does not move. Opening her door for her, Daniel picks her up from the passenger seat and starts to carry her inside, but as soon as he makes contact, with amazing suddenness, she bursts into dry sobs and tries to twist away from him, punching, biting, clawing, fighting to escape. He hangs grimly on: her voice careers into a scream, and Daniel recognises that she is utterly beyond her own control, or his. He somehow manages to get her into the kitchen and to sit down, pulling her against him to contain her struggling, managing to clasp together her two hot hands in one of his to stop her scratching and tearing, his right leg hooking awkwardly around her ankles, his left arm, against which she strains desperately, clamped across her waist. Every atom of both their energies contributes for some moments to maintaining this delicate equilibrium, while Ilona keeps up an almost steady screaming, which, as she loses strength, drops into hysterical weeping in which one word is occasionally intelligible, 'Home – home – home,' her breath coming in irregular rasping gulps. Then it is as if panic bursts in Ilona's head, as if she caves in on herself. If she wants to stop, apparently she cannot. Her small frame subsides, begins to fall.

It is into this scene that the doctor, called by Antoine whose return has gone unnoticed, arrives. Young, dark and smart, swinging his attaché case, he is almost a parody of a medic, calculated to reassure. Ilona sags unconscious between Daniel's knees, his hands under her armpits, strands of hair plastered across her wet and swollen face, her pale clothes damp and stained. Droplets of blood stand out in little rows on her forearms. The lightness with which she is now able to be handled astonishes Daniel, who has felt in danger of being overcome by her sudden strength. The doctor loosens her clothes, sits her on the edge of a chair, with her head on her knees, inert, and then, when she comes round, picks her up and carries her through to her bed, asks Daniel for a towel to put underneath her head, and lays her gently down. He asks, 'What happened?'

Persuaded to leave her for a few minutes, that now she will be alright, Daniel, in the kitchen, tells what he knows. The doctor says that she is extremely thin, that her blood-sugar seems to have been very low (he has given her glycerine), and Daniel agrees that she has barely eaten since her mother's funeral, although he has tried, even putting his arm around her and feeding her, bringing a spoon to her mouth. 'Is it the first time something like this has happened?' The first time to that extent, Daniel says. 'And she's lost her mother?' The doctor writes on his pad, not a prescription but the names of two specialists, a paediatrician and a psychiatrist.

*

'I was in a lay-by', Ilona will tell Dr. Echs. Asked how she got there, she dips her head and doesn't want to talk about it. He prompts, 'There was a lorry-driver? Had he given you a lift?'

There is no answer and her eyes begin to dart around the room behind the doctor's chair, he can read on her face although not on her lips the word 'trapped'; she is ill at ease, beginning to be physically uncomfortable, too warm, heart beating fast. Dr. Echs says, benignly, 'You'll tell me another time'. Ilona looks up at him, to gauge the value of this promise or prediction on her behalf.

*

'You think she might have been abused by the guy in the lay-by?' asks Dr. Echs. 'Or that she got a lift with someone on the way and...?'

'There didn't seem to be any sign of it,' says Daniel, for Ilona underwent in his presence an examination, the doctor shining a light and looking without touching before taking a superficial swab, and glancing discreetly at her backside, too, Daniel had noted, when he got her to lie on her side for an injection, a tranquilliser. Then he sat her in the bath and told Daniel to run a jet of warm water all over her, soothing; the tears still came but she was quiet, and, once dried and put into bed, sank into sleep, lying half on her stomach, diagonally across the mattress, one arm flung out, filling the empty space.

*

An hour or so after midnight, Daniel sees the lights of a car snaking down the narrow approach road, announcing a visit from two policemen, who claim to be following up a call concerning a man seen driving off from a lay-by with a distraught young girl; it happens that the number of Daniel's car has been given. Would the young girl in question be his daughter? Is everything alright? Daniel, who is shaky, grey with fatigue and who hasn't shaved since leaving Canada, asks them into the kitchen, in which Ilona's distress is still to him heavy in the air, although the room has physically been tidied. He explains, he fetches the solicitor's documents still in his holdall, he shows the doctor's note for the paediatrician. These are duly inspected, without any visible shift in attitude. The two men seem impassive, unimpressed. They ask if they can see Ilona. Daniel explains that she is now asleep, but leads them nonetheless down the passage to her room. He has left the door open to be able to hear if she should wake. The three of them, almost absurdly quiet, thinks Daniel, tiptoe to her bedside and stand looking down at her as she sleeps, now foetally curled with her back to them, breathing deeply and regularly. The shutters are still open, the room is swept with moonlight. 'She doesn't like the dark,' Daniel whispers. Her cases still stand by the door; Daniel will move them before he goes to bed so that she will not wake up to this. Back in the kitchen he explains that they have just arrived from Canada, yes, today, that very afternoon. He is asked to sign a paper stating that he has been interviewed, and the policemen leave.

Daniel checks on Ilona before he goes to sleep. Softly rearranging her quilt, he nonetheless causes a little shiver, a little wriggle, and she wakes for an instant and says, 'Mamma.'

'Shhh,' he says, folding her in his arms and soothing her until she resettles, and, for sheer exhaustion, making his way instinctively under the quilt and falling asleep with an arm around her waist.

*

'Sweetheart,' says Daniel, sitting on the edge of the bed, not sure whether he is connecting. Ilona is technically awake, her eyes are open, but she lies on her side, looking blankly out at the room, or rather, perhaps, looking inward. 'I've made an appointment to see the paediatrician this afternoon,' he tells her.

Mindful of his mistake of the previous day, he sits her up, holds the orange juice he has brought in for her to sip, starts to run her a bath, undresses her and bathes her as if she were three, continuing to talk, about the weather, about how they will drive into Nice that afternoon. She is floppy and lethargic, and he carries her out onto the *terrasse* where there is a hammock, settles her on this, and feeds her apple compôte with a coffee spoon, swinging her very gently. 'Good – girl,' he says as she finishes the pot. He asks her whether she would like to read or be read to, and she shakes her head.

'Sweetheart,' he says again, 'you're going to have to say something, so I know you still can.' When she opens her mouth to try, a rusty little sound comes out, she pushes, hard, forcing air, as if her capacity for speech really were in doubt – and indeed her throat must be raw from the screams of the previous evening – and then he sees that she is at the stage where any attempt at speech means tears. He thinks that tears would be better than this stony distance, and so he persists. She finally manages, 'I can't,' and then dissolves. But he recognises this as a step back towards him: she burrows into his lap as if she is trying to get inside his body with him and soaks a patch of his trouser-leg with tears.

*

The drive into Nice is both a release for Ilona and a further alienation. Although she is scared of the strange house, refusing to touch it or to make bonds, and relieved to be away from the need to do so, the utterly unknown country around is even more disconcerting.

Filling in Ilona's file, Daniel feels once more defensive, as if judgements are about to be passed concerning his improbable passage to parenthood. In the consulting room, Ilona does not sit down but leans against Daniel as if for support or protection; his arms close around her waist and he shifts her to one side while he explains, confirms the doctor's report from the previous evening, and hands over the copy of her medical record which he has thought to have made in Canada. The paediatrician questions Ilona courteously: how does she feel? Is there any pain? Ilona shakes her head. She is asked to undress to her underwear; Daniel thinks too late that a mother would have thought to see that she had on something pretty. As it is she is, as often, in brushed cotton jeans and a jersey top, but she has just a pair of plain white pants underneath. Somewhere in her luggage are little sets with matching cropped tops, decorated with flowers or bees or hearts.

She is measured, weighed, her pulse and blood pressure taken, her tongue, eyes and ears examined. The paediatrician produces a chart from his desk with girl's bodies of varying weights and proportions drawn on it, and asks her to go and look at herself in the mirror in the corner and then tell him which of these girls she thinks she most resembles. He notes but does not comment on her response, and tells her she can get dressed. He also notes that she seems confused, is slow to remember where she has put her clothes, and that Daniel helps her, pulling her top over her head and combing her hair back into place with his fingers.

The doctor takes an ecography and tells them, making much of it, almost congratulating Ilona, that she is physically perfect, that she has a beautiful pair of kidneys, and prescribes Eleutherococus and Escholtza, for what he terms, kindly euphemistic, her little problem. He stresses that it is absolutely essential that she put on weight. He sends her into the waiting room, and tells Daniel that he hardly needs to examine her to see that things are not as they should be. Daniel says that she was much better while they were still in Canada, that she seems to have given up completely, shut down. That she ran away almost on arrival, although some of her animus toward him seems to have worked itself out overnight. Nonetheless, leaving, he feels vaguely accused.

It is only some days after their arrival at Ste-Marie that Daniel realises with shock that he has exceeded his agreed absence from the office, which seems unreal, a world away. He phones Max, with whom he has not been in touch in the whole of his time in Canada. As far as Max is concerned, there is no Ilona, Daniel having supposedly seen to the arrangements concerning her life elsewhere, made his excuses and left.

Max and Daniel collaborate on legal scenarii in films, and sometimes in real life. Max is American, and carefully cultivates a sometimes vicious frankness. When Daniel calls Max to tell him about Ilona, they end up shouting within ninety seconds. Max says Daniel can't just spring this on him. Daniel says that actually if it comes to that he'd written on his application papers before signing his first contract, way back before the partnership, that he was party to a hypothetical adoption agreement. Max says Daniel has no idea what he is doing. Daniel says it is then his sexuality that is at stake, and that Max and his wife, man and woman, haven't succeeded too well on the child-rearing front. Max has a fifteen-year-old son at an expensive English boarding school who has greatly suffered from his parents marital holocaust.

Later the same day, Max, always volatile, calls back and says he thinks they can work it out. He asks what the child's name is: Ilona Cécile.

'Ilona? Isn't that a Scottish island?'

'No, not Iona, Ilona: Hungarian. Hestia chose the name years before she was born, she just liked it, plucked it out of the air.'

'How old is she?'

'Ten.'

'And has she been given any choice in all this?' continues Max, with the emphasis on the *she*. Meaning Daniel has not, is what he suspects is the implication of this remark. Daniel notes this but does not feel ready to answer the charge.

'Apparently, she wants what her mother wanted for her. Anyway, what choice is there? She's not a stray dog. There are no Good Homes.'

'And do you have a get-out clause?'

Daniel says they haven't, at this stage, decided whether it's to be a legal adoption or a guardianship. But that if it really doesn't work out – . This sentence he cannot finish. Max sees that for Daniel this just isn't a possibility.

'I didn't know that you really wanted a child – it's kind of a surprise –'

After a silence Max begins again. Adopting a child of ten – what about pubescence? What if he has a Lolita on his hands?

'No Lolitas,' says Daniel, who believes he is not programmed to fall in love with pre-pubescent girls. After some inconclusive discussion about practical arrangements, Max faxes through a proposal for what he calls a 'package'. Daniel is to take six weeks, backdated from his return from Canada, with no demands from the office at all. When the six weeks are up, he will work on the most important cases, at home, coming into Nice only when necessary. When Ilona starts school, Daniel will be back in the office as much as her timetable allows, freeing himself for late-nighters when necessary. Daniel says he has a great many arrangements to think about, puts down the phone, and wonders if he wants his life arranged.

Ilona requests a swing, in the garden at Ste-Marie, and Daniel rigs one up, hanging from the plane tree, a plank with a rough hole at each corner, knotted rope. She sits in this for hours every day, her only activity, scraping out a shallow dip beneath with her feet as she passes, sometimes violently – thin legs stuck out straight in front of her, whooshing up until she is almost horizontal – sometimes gently, hypnotised by the movement. Sometimes Daniel stands in the doorway of the kitchen, watching, and, in silence she watches him back.

VI

In the beginning, during the days at Ste-Marie when Ilona breaks down completely and simply exists, without volition, having to have everything done for her, Daniel will find her curled in the furthest corner of her bed, right in the apex, against the wall, trying very hard not to be; once she slips down behind it and lies in the dark and dusty corner until he finds her.

But the intolerable hours and days at Ste-Marie unwind into weeks, and the movement of time takes on a rhythm. Ilona is coaxed into eating, sleeping, talking, and gradually into little activities, reading or being read to, learning bits of Spanish and Italian from educational programmes and videos, cooking with Antoine's wife, playing with Antoine's tomcat and the lesser felines, of which there are several, half-wild but sometimes willing to parley in return for food.

Habit winds Ilona's paths through the house and, taking courage, she is able to confront less tensely the outside world; the almost daily drives to see Dr Echs become a time also for sitting outside cafés over red Orangina, for looking at the markets and the shops. She ceases to resist the warm caress of the breeze. The blank wall against which she has felt herself slammed, face-first, each morning on waking, is beginning, minimally, to recede. One morning, instead of waiting to be woken — for if left she will sleep and sleep, or pretend to — she appears on the *terrasse* of her own accord, and comes silently to Daniel as he sips his early coffee, telling him wordlessly that she is beginning to be better. Dr. Echs has hoped that this will happen: that something will click inside, making healing begin to be possible.

She takes up all of Daniel's time; there is no space outside her existence. He feels, he imagines, as overtaken as a new mother, yet nothing is left of the resentment of her incursion into his life. He marvels at her, he delights in her: in her strange, straight little female body, filling out a very little now that she is beginning willingly to eat again, in the simplicity of her needs — sleep, food, affection, love — and the inextricable complexities underlying the manifestations of these needs.

Daniel decides to take her to Paris. This is partly to fulfil her previously intense desire to go 'properly', as she says, which he feels sure is still alive in spite of the weeks of the extinction of desire, of lethargy, and partly because he dreads the departure, on holiday, of Dr Echs, to whom Ilona has become extraordinarily and profoundly attached in the few weeks she has been under his care. Dr Echs has warned Daniel that his absence, after so intense a beginning to the treatment, may be taken badly by Ilona, that he must be prepared for this and if necessary redouble his support. However, she is physically stronger now, less fragile although still easily tired, and Daniel thinks the change, the stimulation, will do her good – and possibly himself. They will stay with Richard, a practitioner of holistic massage and psychotherapy, a friend who would, perhaps, have eventually been a serious lover if Daniel had been able to have a serious lover after David's death – which so far he has not.

Ilona is intensely excited by the prospect of the journey, perhaps the journey more than the holiday itself. Driving into and through the night seems to her inexpressibly exciting, and she makes lists of what they will need: bottles of water and a flask of strong coffee, CDs to listen to, puzzle books for her, tissues, sweets to suck. Daniel buys her a beanbag cushion to make the back of the car more comfortable and encourage her to sleep on the way.

Two or three hours out of Ste-Marie, Ilona, who has not intended to sleep but to stay awake to observe the stars and the dark spaces of the night and the cars streaming past the other way, wakes with a start as Daniel slows down and stops the car by a field. She has been dreaming of her mother, and comes to muddled and unhappy. Somehow crumpled, still very sleepy, in the back seat, she looks much younger than she is; Daniel, opening the back door and leaning over her to free the clasp of her seatbelt inhales her smell of clean hair and soft skin and pineapple fruit-gums, and is overwhelmed with tenderness. He helps her out, waits for her to stretch, lifts her and sits her on a gate to look up at the milky way, circling the butterfly spread of her narrow hips with his hands to balance her, conscious of what is fragilely contained between them. She knows that she is somewhere, on a road, with Daniel, in the night, and is content. She gives a little start, rocking slightly on the narrow bar, momentarily unsafe, and he catches her firmly and says, 'I've got you.' In every sense, he thinks. My little girl, caught out, caught up. They both tip their heads back like the stems of flowers swaying away from one another, to look up at the infinitely distant trails of stars. Then he kisses her forehead lightly and swings her down.

VII

Ilona wakes up in the back as the dawn breaks and they approach the outskirts of Paris, visible in the distance as a haze of pollution. They stop at a service station, both with that sticky, gritty feeling that travelling through the night will bring, and have breakfast at a lime-green melamine table, scratched and not quite clean, in an almost empty canteen.

They arrive at Richard's, a fashionable three-level attic on the Ile Ste Louis, just after seven, and carry their things up the five liftless floors. Richard, genial, not quite awake, has a second breakfast laid for them on an iron table on the balcony, in the middle of which is sitting, to Ilona's pleasure, a large tabby cat, unperturbed by their arrival. The view over the city is breathtaking: Paris, really, at last, thinks Ilona, exhaling hard. Before they have finished the tea, Daniel has walked over to the sofa in the large salon, as if on auto-pilot, too exhausted even to excuse himself, and is asleep almost before he has finished lying down. This leaves Richard and Ilona; she looks down, shy, feeling for the first time tacked on to Daniel's existence, not knowing his friends, and feeling, also, slightly panicked: he has deserted her, what to do now? And she knows it is not just the journey that has tired him to this point, it is her... Ilona, waif, stray, refugee, hijacker of his tranquil sad existence. Richard, seeing that she is ill at ease, takes her up to the top of the house, where her bed will be on a chaise-longue under the eaves, shows her the bathroom, and says she might do well to sleep a little, too. He brings her up a *tisane*, not because he thinks she wants it but to reassure her of his presence, to help her settle in, and sits on the chair by her bed stroking the cat, which has wandered peaceably upstairs, to inspect the luggage. Ilona wonders what Richard has and hasn't been told about her, but his voice is soft, his eyes are kind, and the side of the chaise-longue rises up in a great curve, protecting, and she cannot, now, resist sleep.

*

When Daniel and Ilona take the metro, next day, immense swirls
and swathes of undulating colour catch Ilona's eye, posters for a
Munch exhibition, temporarily at the *musée d'art moderne*, where
Daniel agrees to take her.

It is as if Ilona is drawn inevitably towards *The Scream*, as if she
knows what she needs to see, albeit not why, not even skimming the
rooms they pass through, but making her way as if drawn
magnetically to the centre. It hangs between two other similar but
less perfect paintings, *Anguish* and *Despair*, in which the people,
under similarly cacophonous skies, are more realistic and
individual, less simply and devastatingly allegorical than the
wavering swooning open-mouthed foetal figure, hands to ears, on the
edge of physical collapse. Or screaming in disbelief?

The Scream, Daniel informs his charge, is a painting which has
to be seen, which is unduly adulterated in reproduction. It does not
consist of sallow ochre eddies, the land is not sepia, the fields, if
such they are, are not beige-green: there are dark but striking
emeralds and ultramarines in the original where you never would
have guessed at them, with streaks in the canvas left apparently
bare. Ilona compares a postcard, sagely, and nods, impressed.

'It's very small,' she says, and indeed it is many times smaller
than the posters which have summoned them hence.

'But very overwhelming,' says Daniel. 'The painting itself is a
strikingly audacious mix,' he translates for Ilona from the exhibition
notes. '*The Scream* is the more piercing in its aphonic
sempiternality,' – 'Sempiternal means forever,' Daniel tells Ilona,
who says, 'I know,' – 'transmitted through the silent fixed surface of
paint. There is neither the nightmarish, blank, frozen quality of
Anguish, nor the more rooted reality of the hunched clothed person
in *Despair*, although what is disquieting in all three pictures is the
advancement of the figure or figures into the unimaginable off-
canvas foreground, the sense of motion beyond volition, of figures
impelled unstoppably into doom, damnation, chaos.'

Ilona nods, apparently unsurprised.

The space in front of the painting, which is considerable, is
occupied, not physically, but by the acutely possessive gaze of a
woman seated in front of it, and drinking it in as if to get an eyeful
for a lifetime. How many people, wonders Daniel, in how many

countries, have sat or stood in horrified fascination, and known, this is the only painting I ever want to see? This scream, in all its faded jaded clichéd reproductions, echoing down the dusty ignored corridors of how many lives?

In an adjacent bay hang two lithographs of *The Scream* in progress, in black and white, partly coloured in. In these versions, the face shows up much more sharply as a face with features, and the eyeballs are clearer. In the painting proper, the eyes of the screaming figure look almost like empty sockets, sightless.

There is a group of young, surprisingly young, children, visiting the museum, sitting cross-legged in rows on the floor. None can be more than five. One little boy starts to cry and says that he is frightened. Damn right, thinks Daniel, and wonders whether bringing them here was a good idea.

The staring woman suddenly says, to Daniel, in the stillness, 'That's what I came to see. *Homesickness.*'

Daniel looks vaguely around – *Anguish*, *Despair* and *Melancholy*, but he cannot see *Homesickness*.

'Oh – I meant *The Scream*. Standing in front of it I forget that it's really called something else.'

Ilona stands looking too, in awe and wonder, placing herself in a direct line behind the woman's chair, as if this person's rapt attention could absorb some of the radiation from the picture's impact. She herself is not anxious to come under this woman's gaze.

*

Later, over lunch on a barge, with Ilona apparently delighted by a croque-Madame with runny egg, she says, 'What about the parents, in that painting. Are they walking away from the daughter or catching up?'

Daughter, thinks Daniel. Parents. Allegory to her comes so naturally she doesn't even know she's doing it. 'Maybe we don't have to know,' says Daniel. 'Maybe you can take it both ways.'

But through the long afternoon in the Tuileries, and halfway up the Eiffel Tower, and just after she has had her portrait drawn by the Seine, under Notre Dame, she comes back to it: the foetal swooning tadpole-headed figure, is it screaming because it has to live, or die? The boats, tiny in the background: coming in or sailing away?

Hestia

VIII

This is how Ilona was conceived.

The Balham house stretches out kindly in the evening sun, in its solid suburban grace. Dinner is to take place outside. The spaces of and around the house are generous; the front door, central to the façade, gives on to a gravelled driveway; at the back, French windows stretch into the garden. The lawn sprawls, enormously wide and long for London, down to the common. The trees are tended, the borders beautifully landscaped, planted with flowers imported from Holland. Behind a low red-brick wall towards the bottom of the garden, cracked and covered in creepers, there is a pond with frogs, which, surprised, will shoot spectacularly off their lily pads and disappear. Cats wander. There is something quintessentially English and familiar about the house, Hestia thinks, sitting sun-warmed on the steps with tea, although none of the people who live here is English and they do not constitute a family, Daniel and David, who have the rooms on the second floor, Yan and Rudi, who have the first. The ground floor – velvet drawing room, dining room with old pine and rubber plants, kitchen with range, pantry, utility room – is shared.

Hestia longs, as every time she visits, to make contact with the place, for the past the house has accumulated, with its vast lining of books, paintings, photographs, bric-a-brac, to be her past. Yet at the same time, the contact she makes with the surfaces of the house fills her with unease. Suspicions lurk in spite of herself. Dirt. Germs. Sex. Something potentially transmissible which can't always be packaged into the neat and dangerous boxes of HIV or herpes and thus reduced to biological improbability. She assumes they are careful, Daniel and David, Rudi and Yan; they all seem to want to live. And David is a doctor, and presumably knows the risks. One of their friends had said to her, once – a beautiful, wasted man, visiting, – 'What the hell makes you think you're so special? What gives you the right to live when others die? For God's sake get out there and have sex. I don't regret it.'

Where Hestia came from, social and sexual cackhandedness was apparently the path to salvation; refusing to assume even the thinnest veneer of worldliness. As 'a drink' in that house was a glass of orange squash, so any manifestation of sex or sexuality was indecent. Those, dropping in extremely rarely, who might require or expect something more from the daughters on either front inspired confusion and resentment, and invariably, reproach. There was innocence of a sort: a refusal to acknowledge the badness of the world, the danger, particularly the sexual danger.

This unease has continued, more or less, through the decade of her friendship with Daniel. First love, or at least, her love, then friendship. It is an unease which she can live with, which she has had to learn to live with, because ever-present. Perhaps it is herself she experiences as dirty, guilty. Certainly she is afraid of her body, of what might be lurking in those inaccessible depths like some sort of Loch Ness monster. Her own fear of herself she has come to admit, and this adnission allows her mind, usefully, to throw a web of voluntary and involuntary connections over all sorts of episodes, but she also feels a constant vulnerability to some abstract threat of contamination. Over the years she has come to terms with the fact that she knows, or knows that there is something to know, about what she considers the dark side of Daniel's existence. It is as if the house itself had spoken to her. The hours he keeps, a distant door banging in the night, the messages on the answerphone. She has come to understand that being gay, for Daniel, is not a matter of sexual orientation, but a way of life. A club. It was not always like this – all through Durham, secrecy, discretion, intimate games of dissimulation, had prevailed – but has certainly been so since the move to London. She does not seek admittance. For her it is something Proustian, a shadowy demi-monde; he is Odette de Crécy, sliding in and out of obscurity. Hermes, slipping between borders, from one world to another.

Hestia is scared of what Daniel brings back with him, intangibly, sex and illicitness and dissolution; and of other things, more tangible: infection, death.

She had heard, the previous evening, something moving through the dark downstairs, reminiscent of the house cats, navigating their near-silent way among the dusty gold stars – stars stencilled, beautifully and improbably, on the blackened floorboards. Daniel, back from one of his forays into the Hades of the West End, not long before dawn, scaring her in spite of herself: there was no rationalising it, her heart was racing, racing... . She had looked out over the garden, at the lawns and the rosebushes in the moonlight, the common beyond, listened to the terrifying and exhilarating abandon of trains rushing through the night. Then she had locked herself into her room, turning the key, quiet, anxious not to be detected in her fear, standing behind the door, underneath the picture that hung there; six stickmen with jutting spiky penises, and a woman, as on an operating table, skirts dragged up and back...

Summoning strength, trying to be reasonable, she had let herself out of her room, out of her terror; faced him in the pale light at the top of the stairs, looking for once down into his eyes. His pupils were dilated, huge; he had taken something; he took it to be able to − . He had kissed her lips lightly and passed on; had barely registered her presence, he was in another world. She had wiped his kiss off her lips, gone over its imprint, distracted, with a face-cloth in her room.

She was filled with a deep disquiet. She would have liked to have had a bath, but she had already had two that day; hopeless anyway to try to wash it away... Flesh is filthy, little matter whose flesh; and what is she herself but flesh?

She both does and does not want to know how he disposes of his flesh. It started as a young girl, with curiosity, alive and probing, not morbid; she wanted to know, with her mind and her cunt and the tips of her nipples, what two boys did when they were together, fascinated. And then later, when she was in a position to be told, for information once X-rated to go uncensored, she would cover up her ears, shrink into herself in spasm. Damn it with biblical epithets, choking on them, Sodom and Gomorrah. But still a part of her most desperately wanted to know, and it was this, perhaps, that made her body shut everyone out: the secret awareness that part of her craved knowledge, and that knowledge was defilement. And at the same time another part refused such knowledge to the point of spasmophilia, of throwing up, of crying in bed with the quilt wrapped around her tightly, tightly, access to all orifices denied.

Cleanse me with hyssop and I shall be clean, wash me and I shall be whiter than snow....

It was not unease but the knowledge that she must not trespass that had eventually driven her out of the Balham house; that and the fear of Daniel asking her to go. She had wondered whether a point had to be made: she must not be felt to impose a strain on the relationship between Daniel and David. Anyway, she could not stay in the long term; this is a place she visits, but it is not her place. I have left a life of exile, Hestia had thought, to find more exile in London, ostensibly the womb tucked against the beating heart of the country to which I am supposed to belong.

For several years she had lived in France, in a province she now thinks of as distant and foreign to everything except itself, although comfortable, cosy. What had made her come back to England was a very definite sense of closure, of parts of her life completing themselves and folding up around her, easing themselves into flat-pack boxes and piling up in corners, waiting to be transported. A three-year analysis, she believed at that time, finished. Her doctorate completed – even the extra eighteen months for adaptation before publication had elapsed. Her laconic affair with Pierre, burnt out and finally pointless, and over as if nothing had ever been: no common apartment, no child, not even a shared car. There was a growing flock of people around her, meeting, marrying, each other or outsiders, leaving. Hestia was a little over thirty. She decided to go back and look for a lectureship. Why here, she had thought, and not there? I could be having a good time.

So far she is not.

Nonetheless, Hestia was sick of Strasbourg. She was sick of dog-shit smeared all over the streets, even on the pedestals of post boxes and, seasonally, under the Christmas trees in the squares; sick of getting an inevitable slice of ham on her green salad, and of being called Mademoiselle and not Doctor. Sick of her qualifications going unrecognised and underpaid when her mind felt like a racehorse ready to go, sick of French pseudo-intellectualism and of its puppets who thought they spoke English better than she did, sick of hearing strings of clichés, generally slightly mangled, pass for conversation from the lips of academics whose absorption of the concept of the interlocutor as co-enunciator was so complete that whether their listener got one solitary word in edgeways struck them as inconsequential.

One of them wrote thus to his publisher, asking Hestia to read his letter through: 'I am writing to lay the project of a book before you. I have published an article in a widely-read French journal, and the response on the part of the scientific community at large was so enthusiastic that I decided to extend my research on the subject.'

And the subject in question? An AIDS breakthrough? A blueprint for peace in the Middle East? A cure for fascism in the twenty-first century? No: 'Betrayals of the postmodern (aesth)ethic in a surprising number of contemporary British novels'.

Perhaps a little flowery, and maybe *the* betrayal, said Hestia when asked, to have her word, flowery, thrown out, and her advice ignored.

Hestia was also sick of institutionalised sexism and con-descension, of being told that she didn't have a career because she was not a civil servant. She laughed in the face of their *mouvement nationale*, which sounded like a mass bowel movement, at their points for getting married and getting pregnant and having children (ninety per item), at the great ambition of the French functionary to get posted back to his or her home town. But she was also sick of being paid by the hour, of always being the last in the department to be considered, and had learnt how very unlike taking a vacation it is to be a *vacataire*, a sessional lecturer...

But what ran counter to this was the fact that she was caught permanently between two stools: taking refuge in English literature, English newspapers, English coffee mornings, but shocked by England when she went there, with its bizarre train service and its lack of health care and its colour supplements on penis shape and size in women's magazines and advice on how best to practise bestiality. She lived in the state of Betwixt and Between. It was like the rings, yellow and green, the yellow pulling back to where they come from, the green pulling away. In England, Hestia used to be pulling towards France – so, away from her origins – in everything she read, the films she saw, the food she chose to eat – and in France, it was always the other way, pulling back to where she came from through the cultivation of her own English enclave: *The Guardian*, Graham Greene – because he was there in all the libraries and bookshops, Marks and Spencer's' food...

When one acquaintance, whom happiness made cruel, had asked Hestia, what have you got in Strasbourg, why do you want to stay?, she had answered unflinchingly: the illusion of belonging.

But why in God's name, she had asked herself, periodically and then daily, do you even imagine you belong to Strasbourg? A handful of familiar faces? Whose are those faces, those masks? People who you bump into in the street, people who call your name...

And had formulated it, finally, thus: in Strasbourg I have looked loneliness in the face and stared it down.

Strasbourg is full of the flotsam and jetsam among which Hestia counted herself; some leave, some stay. Anne came from England, stayed a year, then two, and said, why stay, what have I to stay for? But left and phoned Hestia, saying she was lonely, so very lonely; went, in due course around the world, got married, had a baby. And still said she was lonely. Silke had stayed for more years than she lived where she came from, and her endless chain of boyfriends, more than one of whom beat her up, seemed to Hestia simply pointless. She stayed, with no job, no income, no children, but never seemed to think of leaving. American Patsy stayed long enough to get bitter and to lose the strength to go anywhere else, hating her husband, hating the French system, mocking Hestia's youth and optimism, so that she felt corrupted. Hannah, happily married for forty years, would doubtless die there, and wouldn't want it any other way. And weirdest of all, Christine, who used to be French, spent twenty years in England before coming back to Alsace, and became English. This had nothing to do with documents declaring nationality: she actually became English, English became her first language; she was the only person Hestia had ever known with a truly adopted mother tongue. People who think they speak their second language without an accent were nothing on this. Christine was a changeling, a throwback in her own lifetime...

Now that Hestia has left, her furniture from Strasbourg, the trappings of expediency rather than of choice, sits, the pieces discreetly and compactly turned in on each other, in the cellar of the Balham house, but Hestia has moved to live with Sven, who has a house, a much less spacious, less elegant house, a few roads away, and who needed a lodger.

At one time, years ago, for the first few terms in Durham, the three of them had gone round together, within the enclosure, at the time so full of daunting possibility, in retrospect so endearingly narrow, of lectures, seminars, tutorials, libraries, college, the boat club, the bar. Daniel had been the pivot in the triangle: Hestia and Daniel, Daniel and Sven. Hestia had loved Daniel, and for a time, a much shorter time, Daniel had more or less secretly loved Sven. Sven had had a girlfriend, Paula, who had seemed to Hestia and sometimes to Daniel pretty much interchangeable with the host of other somewhat horsey public school girls by whom she was surrounded, in her college on the hill.

In spite of this, in time the outer points of the triangle had joined: Hestia and Sven. Not a great deal had happened. What did happen happened in a still-drunken June dawn after one of Daniel's parties, a bonfire on the river bank, far out of the city. At bottom this encounter had been a matter of displacing energy, completing a pattern, although there had always been a flirtation, independent of the need for formal satisfaction. They did not go so far as to sleep together, for this was the code of student infidelities in that somewhat conservative place and at that newly puritanical time. Hestia relied on this being understood. In fact she had not actually gone so far as to sleep with anyone; although sometimes she felt she went further, through trying to find ways out of it and round it, and would then feel sullied. She had developed a strong line in diversionary tactics, and besides that, poured out, quite effortlessly, endless verbal stimulation. Or titillation, which is how she thinks of it now. Unhealthily wrung out with desire. Sven, whose style in those days was aggressive and melodramatic, had physically ripped her shirt off, among the overhanging leaves of summer trees, under a generous moon, and Hestia had kept the torn cheesecloth as a sort of private trophy, a prize awarded to her sexuality as she clocked up prizes for her academic work, from both college and department. She did not consider then that she had been selfish or frigid, merely that she had withheld something which was, understandably and legitimately, to be saved for later. For when things became, she supposed, more real.

This coupling accomplished, even if partial and incomplete, some of the tension between the three of them dissipated. Sven said nothing of the incident to his girlfriend; Hestia told Daniel, and he was, or appeared to be, offhand but amused. She always told Daniel about her sexual adventures, and, occasionally, misadventures. Once a lawyer friend of his had tied her up, and, several days later, considerably more shaken that she had intended, she had shown Daniel the bruises, graduated shades of violet on her thighs, a long mussel-shaped tinge of yellowing mauve inside each upper arm where he had gripped, dark flecks down her back and cheeks, purple turning to green and gold, like mermaid scales. Shrugging it off. Something to prove. Daniel had laughed and commiserated at the same time, pulling her down to the floor and hooking a sympathetic elbow around her neck as they sat. Their own relationship was chaste but not entirely devoid of physicality. Daniel needed to have women around, for social as well as affective purposes, first Hestia, and then later, not only her, by a long way. She had not always been sure of her prestige.

Not long after the event by the riverside, Hestia went away for her undergraduate year abroad and eventually heard, although for a longish period incommunicado in the south of France, busy loosening herself from the certainties of public school and Durham, that Sven had broken up with Paula. When she came back to begin her final year, she found something odd, impenetrable in the atmosphere of the group which had been hers, felt shut out, excluded, without being able to pinpoint as the cause silence on some essential question. This, the return to England after the first long period away, was a brutal homecoming. Her contemporaries seemed to have changed, or perhaps had only stayed the same. Hestia, less sure of herself at college than she realised at the time, was preoccupied with suspicions of her own exclusion, not just by friends but perhaps also academically and professionally, and forever. This was a time of anxiety for her, before she got her First to give her strength. Sven, always to her knowledge moody, was said barely to emerge from the flat he was sharing with a girlfriend, not Paula. Then about a fortnight into the Advent term, Hestia bumped into him in a narrow passage of the pub between the house she shared and his flat. She had been about to kiss him on either cheek, in the French way, a habit which had not yet deserted her, and had for half a second understood that his hand had flown out accidentally, in an effort, it seemed, to regain his balance, perhaps he was drunk or had tripped – but no, he had hit her, had in a public place simply walked up and slapped her in the face. She stood in shock and astonishment as his accusations spilled over her: bitch, whore, nympho, it's all your fault, it happened because of you. She had absolutely no idea what he was talking about, but perhaps, she feared afterwards, those listening in the bar, hovering on the verge of coming to break it up, had. Upset and knocked badly off balance, she had run down to Daniel's, a place of refuge even then, and he had told her, tight-lipped and reluctant, that Sven had tried to kill himself while she was away, that he had written in a note that it was because Paula had left him. Daniel added that Sven blamed anyone and everyone, that he had aggressive outbursts, that she was to take no notice. That he would end up apologising of his own accord.

Hestia had blamed herself for Daniel's coolness and distance, feeling like a child who didn't have the right to know what was going on and had only confirmed what a self-willed little tyke she was by demanding to be told and dragging skeletons out of cupboards to the detriment of everyone involved. At the same time, she had felt unbearably excluded, she, who thought so much of her friends, who had believed herself part of it, not to be told! A nothing-person, reduced to non-function by lack of information. Later, she had come to understand that Sven's aggressivity towards her had coincided with his brutal rejection of Daniel, a calculated and systematic pushing-away. Perhaps it had been because Daniel saved him, or perhaps because Daniel was gay and Sven could not bear to be identified with that, perhaps both or neither, but Hestia had understood some of what Sven had meant to Daniel the day he introduced her to David. David, tall and slim, blond, blue-eyed, like Sven, but all warmth and sunshine where Sven had become bitter and dour. Until the day he had decided to take that warmth and sunshine away.

For the rest of that year in Durham, Hestia had avoided Sven, fairly successfully, making no attempt to throw off the guilt which had been foisted upon her. And even in the throes of leaving, the last formal hall for graduands, Pimms on the graciously sloping college lawns, Sven had not thawed. Why then, now, more than ten years later, was she living in his house? She needed a place to stay, had yearned to come back to something tangible and solid, not days of hasty hunting for an unsatisfactory flat in hostile London. In recent years she had always experienced London as hostile, which meant that, conversely or perversely, it held potential for the degree of alienation she found necessary, to live. There was also, less masochistically, the desire to be near Daniel. And besides, Sven now worked in the city, appeared to have stabilised; he was at work or out most of the time, she saw little of him. Yet stupidly, she had permitted a sexual skirmish with Sven, since being back, she who had been used to limit or curtail these so severely in the years unfolding since irresponsible studenthood. Perhaps she felt that she could trick herself thus into a change of attitude, become a sexual being again, remember how to put out signals and act on them, get a partner, get a life. This encounter, the result of taking a cup of tea into Sven's room one Sunday morning, had started out gentle, nostalgic, and ended with her crying off at the last moment. Sven had called her a fucking bitch and said she hadn't changed.

'What do you know about it?' Hestia had said, nastily, struggling appalled back into her bathrobe – for once it was established that sex was out, Sven had shown no desire to lie and caress her nakedness – but in fact it was true, she hadn't changed, not even with Pierre, who perhaps had reasons of his own for letting this go.

'I know. Everyone knew,' he had replied. She had been unsettled by this. Sometimes she wondered whether virginity was not somehow inscribed in her face, or, more probably, in her body, in its tensions, its lack of graceful spontaneous movement, its tendency, these days, towards stolidity, which she worked hard to counteract. She felt sometimes as if she harboured a sordid deformity, almost a disease. Once, in a Soho café with Daniel, they had bumped into someone he knew, a beautiful woman with long auburn hair, dressed in dramatic high-heeled black: Rose, who, Daniel informed her some time afterwards, 'used to be a man'. This had had the effect of making Hestia anxious to meet her again, to impress, to attract; and at the same time she had not been able to help thinking of what lay hidden under those tight black trousers, and had thought: that's what I'm like. I look like a woman but I'm not, I can't be.

Sven could be very unpleasant – in fact that morning he and Hestia had argued, which is why she is glad to be back at the big house tonight. He had asked her to be out of the house as he was inviting someone, presumably a woman, more likely a young girl, over for dinner. Hestia had said that as she was paying him rent this was a bit steep, but that anyway she was going out. 'You mean you're going to Daniel's,' Sven had said, and then, spiteful, 'It's not as if you ever go anywhere else.'

'I've just got back from France', she had said, placatingly. 'I need a bit of time to get myself together.' They both knew that the crush of London, it's brutal, swaggering anonymity, were sometimes beyond her, everything, as Hestia saw it, in your face (the very language she heard in the streets a prime example), after the slowness, the bourgeois solidities, of Strasbourg. She had come, as every time, with a sense of being braced for adventure, standing on the brink of her real self, and this had petered out, as it always did, with the first jam on the Northern line, the first tense march back from Balham station late at night with her keys clutched between her fingers, ready to strike, the first spaced-out addict encountered in a confined space. The sense of drawing herself into herself for protection was almost physical, a sort of shrinking away from all surfaces, and not just those of the Balham house. A disturbed anemone, pulling in its tentacles. Perhaps this habit was the price to pay for too high a degree of exile, for too long.

This evening, the air in the garden at the big house in Balham feels fresh on her skin, even if it is not. She is invited, for Yan's thirtieth birthday. He is the youngest of the four, he does not want to turn thirty, and the event is to be celebrated quietly. He is the quintessential boy, with close-cropped black hair and dark blue eyes, and hardly looks more than twenty, although incongruously he is a broker in the city. Hestia is nonetheless uneasy at table, as she is often uneasy. The aperitif is brought out and drunk, dishes appear, a stuffed salmon with potatoes and salads. She is aware that a stiffness, a self-watching, resides deep within her, unchanged by the smiling façade of the red brick house, which she reads also as treacherous, or the evening sun, or the circle of the six of them around the table, the two couples, Yan's sister, Hestia herself. Photos are being passed round, Yan and friends in outrageous drag. Hestia is, despite herself, disconcerted. She wants to see, she has been taught to see, carnival, the joyful overturning of gender and type, the schoolboy queen. Nevertheless outward manifestations of sexuality bother her, and she sees without wanting to something worthy of punishment. A few years previously, going through a long, unstable patch, she would see flaming visions of hell all the time, torture and suffering, without even closing her eyes. Like the vestiges of a bad LSD trip, except that she would never dare take LSD. The punishment without the crime, once more. How many other full-time virgins spend their time worrying about catching AIDS and VD, wonders Hestia, wryly. She picks at her food, saying little.

Suddenly, inside, the dogs begin to bark: someone is at the front door. The only way to the garden is through the house, so Yan, supposing that any visitor is most likely to be for him on his birthday, gets up and goes to answer the door. When he re-emerges down the steps from the French windows, it is Sven who follows him out, a bottle in either hand, a double passport to the feast. He stands suspended for a few moments at the top of the steps as the others take in his presence. He has not been invited. He hesitates, surveying the scene, the candles flickering against the dusk, envelopes and scraps of wrapping paper heaped in the middle of the table.

Hestia knows little about Daniel's relationship with Sven these days but has gathered it is not intense. Daniel feels it his duty to check that he is alright, to heed any clang, however faint, of his inner alarm bell, whose toll had saved Sven before from the viscous and bloody death he had elected. He is often met with abuse, much of it targeting David, or Daniel's sexuality in general.

'Well hello', says Daniel, and then, slightly stiff, a fraction too late, 'Would you like to come and join us?' There is little option but to ask. He tips one of the cats off the seventh chair, and goes into the house to get extra plates and cutlery. Sven sets a bottle on the table: not wine but whisky. As the others are already half way through the meal, he is the only one to drink it, which he does, liberally. The party sinks into an awkward silence; everyone begins to ask him or herself why Sven has come, but fairly quickly it becomes apparent that he has come to bother Hestia, and through her, Daniel and the other inhabitants of the house. Hestia's tension has mounted with Sven's appearance. When she gets up to serve him, which seems easier than passing the heavy dishes across the now encumbered table, he tells her sharply to stop mothering him, and then adds nastily, 'Not eating much yourself, are you. Worried you might catch something?'

Hestia ignores this and reflects that even if those present see what Sven is trying to get at, they won't really understand the route of his attack on her, which is too abstruse. She scoops up the cat, which, for once, ejected, has not stalked offended into shadows but has stayed close, and settles it on her lap.

'Why don't you eat something instead of stroking the bloody cat?' pursues Sven. 'Like a little girl. A bloody ageing Lolita.'

This ludicrous remark is made with a heavy, almost a lewd, sneer, and takes a further notch off Hestia's appetite.

'Funny how you can't cope with a man in your bed, but all these fucking poofters getting up each others' arses, that's fine with you, isn't it?'

Sven sees that he has managed to awaken discomfort and is delighted, his aggression feeds on itself and grows monstrous. Hestia says that she will go and feed the cats and sit inside for a little, but Yan, who has spent the afternoon cooking the food and who is beginning to get annoyed, tells her to stay where she is, have another glass of wine, enjoy herself, and mildly suggests to Sven that he should leave. Sven falls silent, but stays put. He does not eat. There are attempts all round to get the evening back on the rails, to launch carefully neutral topics of conversation, to which Sven pointedly refuses to respond. The dinner goes on as it can, and over coffee, Sven, suddenly excessively social and polite, thanks them all for the evening and abruptly disappears.

Later, Hestia and Daniel walk around the garden, which is large enough to lend itself to this. 'Like Jane Austen,' Hestia says. 'Walking in the grounds.'

'That's what you are, isn't it,' says Daniel, 'a character from Jane Austen. You might be happier if you behaved like other women.' It is not the first time he has said this, although sometimes it is E.M. Forster, and Hestia knows which characters he means: Charlotte Bartlett, Harriet Herriton. The first time she had ever spoken to Daniel, on Durham station in his first year, her second, he had been reading *Where Angels Fear to Tread*. She herself favours, glumly, for this purpose, Anita Brookner. Characters locked in on their refined and narrow existences, not touching the world.

'Other women have sex,' Hestia says. She is still rattled.

'I don't know why the hell you don't,' says Daniel. 'You've got all the equipment for it.' Too much, has always been one of her secret fears, flesh stretched taut across where none should be. 'If you let yourself change, there's no reason why it shouldn't happen.'

She has told him why it does not, that she cannot, which Daniel discounts. In the gay world there are tangible solutions to that sort of reticence, the means to which you can acquire, for money. Daniel told her, long ago, that Pierre would leave her if she didn't sleep with him, but the relationship finally shut down anyway, and in the end it was she who left. In the early days, for the first couple of years, which she finds impossibly distant now, they had spent entire days in bed, days of urgency, of hearts beating fast, of leaf-green sheets traced perpetually with sperm. Pierre, then, had liked her line in ever-extended foreplay, in exhibitionism, in sex not oral but verbal. Later her inability, or refusal, had become the bedrock of all his complaints, which were many and constant. Disagreements would come back, always, to the line, 'And it's not even as if you're any good in bed. I mean, not even the minimum service. And to think I've been putting up with this shit for years...'.

Once launched, this could, and did, go on for hours, and she had put up with it, until the day she screamed at him, 'Oh, go fuck your Mother!' She used to be disgusted by his mother on the regular weekend retreats from Paris which she knew better than to contest, large and complacent and wholly occupied with her *arts ménagers* – but who was Hestia to call her self-satisfied? At least his mother had, by definition, fulfilled her female function. She remains frozen in Hestia's mind, ladling out the innards of something or other in a delicious sauce, the way they do in the Norman countryside, and then ostentatiously passing the vegetables over to the foreigner, disapproving of her pale English herbivorous habits. Hestia was sure she knew exactly how things stood. For some reason, this bothered her particularly at table; the nausea and disgust she disclaimed under questioning would threaten to rise up and overwhelm her, especially when the things lurking under the sauces were long and tubular.

Pierre had been stifling, his parents worse, muffled in their irritating ways, with their maniacally regular meals and their layers

75

of pointless clothing, his mother's whole existence given over to keeping all this going. What was worse was that Pierre imitated this, making a full-time job out of what he called the 'maintenance' of his two-roomed flat in Paris, which he carried out badly; Hestia hated the mess of dust and grime and pubic hairs in the bathroom and didn't see, after a while, why she should clean any more than cursorily, for her own habitation, when she came for the weekend. It was, after all, his flat and his mess. He would ask her very seriously whether she realised the work involved in keeping up the thirty two square metres in which he lived, and Hestia would reply that housework was what you did in the spaces between living, not the other way round, which seemed to her unquestionably obvious. It irritated her to distraction to see him taking two hours for lunch, laying the table, pulling three courses from the freezer and stopping after each to heat up the next, watching TV in the middle of the day, folding washing at three in the afternoon, and then inevitably declaring that he simply didn't have time to work – he was supposed to be a freelance scriptwriter, but lived a great deal off his parents – and blaming her for it. He had once asked her what sort of a housewife she would make and had been genuinely astonished when she had laughed. And she had never been able to make him understand that full lunch at home from a set table depressed her, that his domestic arrangements stifled her, killed her desire.

Hestia looks back now on the time with Pierre as a disgusting display of childishness, on both their parts. Him and his everlasting mother; worse, her own equally everlasting need to be indulged as a child, by him. Grotesque, like those horrible advertisements in which toddlers are dressed up as businessmen and made to sit in the boardroom, discussing some product, or some darker inversion of this. There was a sense in which they deserved each other, and in which they were each other's perfect torturer.

Later, there had been Nar, whom she had wanted, truly, for his beauty, of body and of soul, for his limitless oriental good humour; exotic Nar, who had arrived in her bed as if by magic carpet. Now, in the Balham garden, Hestia's thoughts bump up against Nar and come to a halt. The wilder of the two cats crouches in shadow by the pond, watching for frogs, intent, and they stand behind, waiting with her. Daniel can feel in her silence that Hestia is about to cry.

There are times when the subject of her sealed body will tip Hestia into a sort of desperate frustration, when she could howl, when she wants to scream to the sky, why is it that every woman can do it, and not me? Once, dwelling on this in a crowded bus in Strasbourg, she had come within an inch of asking the women around her, straight out, point blank. She had wanted to shout it from the rooftops, in sheer frustration: I am a woman who cannot fuck. I have all the equipment, but I just can't make it, never have made it, never will be able to make it. She believes that at one stage, the time of visions of hell and torture, it sent her mad.

'It's like handicapped people, people in wheelchairs; one day they just get up and walk…', says Daniel. 'You can do it, you've just created some stupid block; you have to put your mind to it, mind over matter.'

'That's a bloody stupid thing to say. It's not my mind, it's my body.' Hestia is almost shouting.

'So just get up and walk, people do it every day.'

Plenty of people don't, thinks Hestia.

'You know,' she tells Daniel, 'I used to have this fantasy, when I was young, almost too young to know anything about sex, of my honeymoon with some guy on an island, always an island, and there I was in this great flowing bridal dress, and he'd take it off and then he couldn't get his thing in. And then for the rest of the night he'd just hold me, and we'd listen to the sea.'

'Your problem is that nothing you say any more makes sense to anyone except your shrink. What do you think a guy like Sven would say to that?'

'What I hate,' she begins again, after a silence, during which one frog has leapt and the cat has not moved, expecting better, 'is the way Sven has to *insist* – .' Her French tics of language are still with her, the sentence is not right, it needs rephrasing.

'Sven just does it to get at you. One mention of sex and you go to pieces, he likes to scare you, he sniffs fear and then he preys on it. It's just a stupid game.'

'So women don't get raped and assaulted, then, there is no danger, it's all just a big fairy-tale to keep us on our toes, is it?' Hestia is beginning to get angry. Fear of sexual predators plays a large part in her existence.

'He's got it wrong,' says Daniel. 'Or at least, partly wrong. He brings it all round to sex because that's how Sven sees women. But it's not just sex, you exile yourself pointlessly, you cut yourself off. You can't grow up if you won't let people in. What the hell is it you're hanging onto, some sort of integrity? What is it you think you've got that's too good for other people?'

Both are conscious that she has wanted in the past to let Daniel in, but that there will never be a time to try. The previous week they had been lying in the sun on the lawn of the big house, Daniel with his back to her, covered at the hips with a towel folded in a narrow band, one arm crossed over his chest, absently rubbing one shoulder as he read, or thought, and Hestia, looking at the long slashing shadow of his spine, the tiny creases in the tanned skin where the waist bent (he was curled up, very slightly fœtal), had said, 'I think you have the most heart-rendingly beautiful male body I have ever seen.'

'What sort of a remark is that?' Daniel had said, not looking at her, and Hestia had said, 'I love you, like I breathe air.' And then been very thankful she hadn't said it aloud.

'I just can't have sex,' she says now, circularly. 'That's all. It hurts, I can't do it, maybe I haven't got a proper hole.' She has said this more than once to an endlessly patient gynaecologist, has over years woven increasingly convoluted variations on it to the analyst he referred her to. But still she can't. Attempts at sex come down to something impossibly large and hot and hard and unwelcome, however much she claims to want it, pushing against dryness, and worse than dryness, hardness, utterly unyielding.

With Nar, they had agreed to leave it a while after they met, partly because the affair was classed by both of them as casual even as it begun, and because more than once during the dozen nights they had spent together over three months she had had her period; also because he was Lebanese, and female virginity before marriage was something from his culture, something he understood. The first three times he had just accepted that they would stop short of penetration. After that she had told him and he hadn't believed her, or had half believed her; she was so hungry for him, so energetic in bed, would pull his clothes off, kiss him all over, drive him crazy swishing her long hair on his inner thighs, then nuzzling. Then they would finish it off manually, he coming all over her breasts, her face, hair, pillow, she going to sleep after he had left – he generally left before morning – leaving her in the musky delicious forbidden smell of it, dizzy, happy, unanchored. Once he had asked her to masturbate for him and had lain between her legs, his hands pushing her thighs apart, as she did. She came, easily, quickly; exhibitionism came naturally to her, the semi-darkness in love with her whiteness, her solid curves. It was always in her bedroom, with dusk then the moonlight coming through the open shutters. The same night, he had stayed until three, watching TV from her bed, while she slept beside him, and before he had left had woken her and come on her as she liked him to; she had felt at once foetal and blessed, a goddess, not Hestia but Danae, bathing in Zeus's golden rain.

Nar was beautiful, dusky, dark; she would endlessly stroke his eyebrows, the densest possible black but very fine, perfect, and his curved Arabic nose; it was like caressing the face of a proud but well-disposed panther. Nar too would purr, or almost, lying on his stomach, smiling, sometimes laughing softly to himself at what she did to him. Then time had run out on them; they had been aware that it would, and soon, since the beginning; and one night, in June, which they had thought might be the last, he had lain beside her, playing with her hair, picking up handfuls of it and holding it back from her face, with a sort of casual tenderness, while they talked, and then he had said, 'I've got condoms, this time. Is that okay?' And she had hesitated, and considered his beauty and the love she had for him in spite of not intending to, and said, 'Yes.'

She had been on top of him. The idea was to pull him inside her. But when she pulled there was no answering push open within; she could feel herself completely closed. Not even closed; it was like pushing against a solid wall with no opening at all. After some fruitless shoving, they had finally rolled over, so that he lay on top of her, she with her legs crossed against his back – she knew that much – and he had attempted again to find her. Hestia, panicked, tried to guide him in with her hand. For a while he thrust away, she thought gallantly, pretending, she supposed, for her sake, his pelvis crunching the small bones of her hand, she couldn't take it out; only the tip of him was inside her.

'Nar – '

Silence; he went on, her face pressed against his shoulder, she could not see his expression. She felt uncomfortable, crushed.

'Nar.' More insistent. She used to call out his name for the sheer joy and surprise of finding him, all unlikely, actually in her bed, and, accustomed to this, he did not respond. He had shifted slightly, about to pour himself out. And it was as she extricated herself that he realised.

'Shit. It was your hand.' He had said something in Arabic, and then again, 'Oh, shit.'

But he came on her stomach in the usual way. And he pulled her to him, before he left, heedless for once of the smell of her perfume on his clothes, looked her straight in the eye and said it didn't matter, that she'd make it, she'd get there, with someone who loved her in a different way. Hestia woke the next morning and cried for him for the first time, as if the whole thing were cancelled out by this failure, as if there had never been any honey-gravel voice in the dark telling her, *'Tu apprends vite, vite,'* never her teeth sinking into his skin; as if she had never stroked the insides of his thighs with hanks of her long thick hair. Never to have another lover like him.

IX

Hestia had cried for two days, then gone back to see her gynaecologist. He had contemplated her, sceptically she suspected, and gone through her notes, aloud. Relaxation techniques... psycho-analysis... no apparent physiological difficulty. He eyed her.

'You know,' he said, 'a lot of women fantasise about being raped.'

This was not precisely what he said, he beat about the bush, but this is where he got to, and Hestia had remembered with a thud a recurrent dream: an elbow, crooked around her neck in the dark, a dragging backwards. Under her eye a nerve twitched.

'Valium?'

Hestia said yes please. He prescribed, also, a lubricant, which, she found at the pharmacy, had been packed in a special little white and gold bottle, not to look medical. The sort of product with which any self-respecting virgin goddess could be proud to anoint herself when the great moment came. The enclosed leaflet explained how like her own secretions this liquid would be, how it would heat immediately to her body temperature, no grains, no lumps, no smell, no taste. Foolproof.

At home she had put this sad little pack on her dressing table and burst once more into tears.

'What goes through your head,' her analyst had wanted to know or wanted her to know, 'when he tries to touch you?'

Silence.

'Penetration, just the idea of it, makes me feel sick. Even tampons. I feel so stupid, so lacking...'

At school, someone had left a box of Tampax in her desk draw, and she had tried, locking herself in an upstairs bathroom for hours and pushing against where she was sore and closed even with the blood flowing out. She had spent the rest of that night throwing up, and been allowed to stay in bed next morning, pale and defeated.

'When he asked you why you were frightened, what was actually in your mind?'

Oh, hell. Infection, disease, death in childbirth, death *tout court*, hell precisely with all its concomitant horrors. 'Pain.'

Later, in her bathroom, curled up on the floor against the bath and not intending to come out, Hestia had in her head the image of kitchen scissors snipping through raw meat, and felt all her abdominal muscles contracting violently against this.

*

Next day, Hestia bought a new notebook and tried to write an answer:

The little pain between my legs makes everything worse and I can't work any of it out. I'm not sure whether it's truly a physical pain.

I can't press my legs together tight enough, can't hold my muscles in for long enough, not forever; I wish I could. I need to be able to.

Suction abortion. Dreams of a scuttling white creature falling out from inside me and shrinking away to nothing. Maybe that creature is me.

When I was little, I had an irrational fear of the hoover, rattling along on its metal base with a canvas bag held up with rusting springs. Not just the noise, but something more sinister. I thought it was called a Three Act Drama. Whenever I made a fuss, my mother would say, don't make a Three Act Drama out of it, and that's what I thought the hoover was, some terrible force of punishment or vengeance.

Trying to hold myself in, to close my legs as tight as they possibly can go – I cannot press them together hard enough – could be to stop something being sucked out. How can this be?

Trying to press my legs together to stop there being a hole.
Stop the excavation.

Excavation is when you ask me questions.

Difficulty with urinating, since it happened with Nar; it's too close to the pain, it reminds me, it makes me feel sick. I do it when strictly necessary, once a day, once a night.

Sometimes, I am aware of this wave of nostalgia for my girl's body — not as baby or as pubescent, but for the time between, soft smooth skin and slim unselfconscious limbs, and no sexuality. Not being aware of the hole. How much I want, now, not to have a hole. A channel for intrusion.

I can't feel calm. I feel as if my body is lodging some terrible thing, some deformity, some monster.

And yet: Nar, come back, don't leave me here like this in this black pit of solitude. Take me out of myself, take me away from the bone-bowers of my body, the prison of my mind, give me a corner of your flying carpet...

*

'Open your legs, nothing's going to fall out!'

This had been a camp instructor, she tells her analyst next day, screaming at her. She had been thirteen. Twelve? Abseiling down a cliff, forced into it, so terrified she couldn't look up or down, could barely move her feet over the rockface in their borrowed walking boots. The photograph shows her, face hidden by the helmet, hanging on for dear life, or for grim death.

She is getting older, now it may never happen. *Let me alone*, she thinks incongruously, calling up dusky skin and a filiform old testament maiden, *that I may go up and down upon the mountains and bewail my virginity...*

X

Hestia is not anxious to go back to Sven's after Yan's party, but she bites back asking to stay the night where she is. Daniel has been talking about the unreasonableness and childishness of her sexual fear, and she walks the short distance back in the dark, alone, her keys tightly enclosed in her right hand, a sharp blade protruding between thumb and forefinger, ready, just in case.

It is only as she lets herself in that she remembers that Sven originally had a date for this evening, hence, possibly, the bottles he had brought to Daniel's – an ironic flourish, emblem of what he will see as failure, if he's been stood up. She will go into the kitchen to make tea; she feels a need for it, she is on edge. London stretches sinister in her imagination, a vast and complex prison; she feels trapped. She needs to get out, out and away, why did she ever come back? In the hall, oldish newspapers are piled on a trunk, waiting to be thrown out. She will take some and read them over the tea: the fact that the disasters they trumpet have thus far had no perceivable effect on her is comforting, and makes her feel less fragile and tenuous, more rooted, less easily destructible. She may have to take half a tranquilliser with her tea, if this anxiety, now generalised, will not be dispelled.

She is just about to switch on the kitchen light when the beam of a passing car sends pale rhombuses shuddering across the ceiling, and she sees, in the second before her fingers function, that Sven is sitting at the kitchen table, and must have been doing so in the dark. Fear makes her start, and in that start she flicks the switch abruptly. Sven has a bottle of whisky planted in front of him, a tumbler, and a bread-knife. She sees his pupils shrink into hard points. For a moment, she cannot speak. He does not look at her. She says, 'Shall I phone Daniel?'

No answer. She approaches, heart racing. 'Sven – don't sit there like that. I'm sorry she didn't come – but – '

Then just as before when he slapped her, years ago in Durham, she feels the shock of the anticipation of attack before she has fully understood that it is to her that it is going to happen. Whatever made her think, she wonders afterwards, that his violence was intended for himself? Before she knows it, he has whipped up and round, throwing his chair backwards, and has her jammed against the wall, awkwardly, in the corner beside the fridge which is shoulder-high, a space too small to hold her comfortably, a space too cramped for her to aim a slap: instead he pushes himself up against her, his face in hers, his breath foul. He is saying, over and over, 'You fucking bitch, you fucking whore.' Wedged in as she is, she has no hope of pushing him away. Her throat arches back in panic as she tries to get away from the smell of whisky, her breasts pushing against his chest, which he seems to takes as provocation. 'Let go,' she begs, her face running with sweat and tears, 'please, please, *please*.'

'I'm not going to let you go,' Sven breathes into her face, 'I'm going to teach you a fucking lesson. You and your fucking sick fantasies.'

Her breathing is out of control. His hand is on the back of her neck and he ejects her from her wedged position, banging her left elbow hard on the corner of the fridge, bruising, scraping the skin. He drags her into the hall – did he want to give her the benefit of a carpet to lie on, she wonders later – throws her down and himself on top of her, tearing her top back over her head so that she feels as if she must suffocate, and her arms are in effect pinned back, painfully catching an earring, and scrabbling at the waist of her skirt, giving up and dragging it up instead. He skews her knickers to one side and rips while she screams into her hooked-back top, and then she begins to feel him, butting hard, hard, where she is closed and dry, forcing his way where no one has been, driving himself in. The pain is blinding. She feels herself tear, and hears her own scream rise higher, out of control. Then the crushing weight rolls off her, she struggles out of the trap of her own clothing, and crawls blindly down the hall, to her handbag, to her telephone, weeping so profusely she is barely able to see; she is truly hysterical.

She presses Memory for Daniel's number. Into the pain of which she seems to be wholly composed trickles the awareness of warm liquid rushing, not seeping, down her thighs. 'Daniel, Daniel, Daniel,' she says into the void. The number rings and rings. When he answers she is barely able to make herself understood. 'Just come,' she sobs, 'David. And David. Just come, quick, oh, quickly.'

They come the short distance in the car to pick her up. There is no question of her staying in that house, although Sven has disappeared. Back at the big house, David says he can examine her, for evidence, and she is distraught, does he not believe her? From the state of her, shaking, hyper-ventilating, face scratched, hair pulled down, blood on her legs, anyone can see that it is true. There is a sort of black humour in the reception of this act, the lawyer and the doctor. Against their advice, she insists on taking at once a very long warm shower, on more or less being carried from the bathroom and put to bed with tea; it is very late now as she had already delayed going home. Dawn is beginning to break over the garden; it is almost another day.

David gives her a generous dose of tranquillisers, and they both sit on the side of her bed, holding her hands, stroking her hair. It is the last time, she thinks confusedly, that she will be put to bed as a little girl, the end of all that forever. The amiable clutter of the Balham spare room imprints itself indelibly on her mind in the space before unconsciousness. A framed photo of two men in t-shirts and battered panamas with a zebra, a box of Darkie toothpaste with a stylised grinning native, a registration plate saying LOVE, a bottle of beer with a Russian label, a fawn bakelite alarm clock set at twelve, miscellany running on and on along the shelves. When she has dropped into the abrupt sleep that follows shock, Daniel and David sit in the kitchen, talking over whether she should press charges, and whether she will be able to do so, after the shower. Daniel, who fears for Sven, has been down again to the house but has not been let in. Sven is not answering the phone.

Hestia sleeps on.

*

She had woken, in spite of the sleeping tablets, in the very early dawn, with pain gnawing between her legs, and not, she knew, only there. The sheets, she guessed before putting the light on, were smeared with blood. She was aware without thinking about the rationale of it that she would have to go away, not for a time but forever; she read the rape as a sign. London was no good for her, she should never have come, it could not be made to work. Long ago, all the portents had said, go away and go forever, and she had had the temerity to come back, to consider that she had done her time, purged her pain. When of course it was forever, a life sentence. She felt faced with her own naked self as never before.

She did not know at the time that this was Ilona's conception. Very shortly afterwards she applied for and got a lectureship in Canada. It was from there that she wrote to Daniel that she was pregnant, that only one occasion could have made this possible, that she had decided to keep the child. By the time this was known, Sven had succeeded in killing himself.

XI

The exile's only story is how she came into her exile.

Hestia's story in Canada takes place in the wasteland, after love and after hope. It is about living without, about a set of people who do this.

Once more, thinks Hestia, flying out of London, she has done it; once again, she has burned her boats. She thinks of other times, when there was somewhere to go back to. Staying so many years in France, where she did not belong, had been to do with having established somewhere in Strasbourg to go back to and being unable to give that up, even if on most of her cross-channel journeys she had not known whether she was coming or going...

Hestia has always needed to prove the world to be navigable. As a child she would feign illness to avoid being sent away on camps and Bible weeks, calculating the days and hours to be gained before being packed off all the same, and then her mental calendar would start again at those to be got through. She even now has a horror of trips with fixed return dates you cannot advance, of being in any place she does not know how to get back from. Trips away, holidays, tend to be a matter of pain to her, will stress her unduly. Once she had gone to spend a week in Italy, the week her students were in exams, before the marking, and had been seized after two days in Naples with a totally reasonless and all-consuming fit of homesickness, and had had to go to great lengths to get a seat on a British Airways flight home (then in England), leaving irrecuperable amical devastation in her wake. And because she shrank from explaining this to anybody, she had been obliged to hide out in London for several days, with friends to whom she had not mentioned the trip to Italy. She had left all her Italian souvenirs in a café, as if by accident; this getting-rid of the evidence was another part of the ritual. It was not that any of it mattered, Hestia had concluded at the time, and afterwards – just that she seemed to be turning into a very strange person. Or at least a person who did very strange things.

She will plan, pack, intend to travel, and then at the last moment be incapacitated by doubt, ask herself if her journey is really necessary, as in the war; will anything happen if she doesn't go? It would be so much easier not to than to face the alien desert. She will fail to fly from air terminals and, putting everyone to great trouble, end up going backwards through them where no backtracking is supposed to be possible, as relieved to see the normality of WH Smith and Costa Coffee and The Body Shop as if she had been away for months, so great is the pitch to which she has worked herself up. The need to get back almost immediately from anywhere she goes is, she supposes, born of the desire to return to some tenuous idea of the stable self, which in fact has never existed. She knows the symptoms of this syndrome and the stages of its processes by heart, but almost always recognises them too late, will give way in a panic, and end up curled, foetal and defeated, on her bed, feeling, after the first wave of pure relief, perversely flat and depressed, as if all means of escape have been barred forever, as if she will never go anywhere, ever again. The moves she makes willingly tend paradoxically to be enormous ones, lock, stock and barrel. She had known, moving to France, that she would stay for years, and now, transferring herself to Canada where she has never been, she feels that she may never come back, to live.

And in a panic she wants to turn round and run for home, real home, like her child-self homesick for parents, childhood, suburban gardens. She can see herself before the empty, silent shell of her parents' house, beating on the door with bleeding fists and screaming, Let me in...

The vision is so unbearable that, finally, she smiles: conjuring it up has made her glad to leave. She knows now that homesickness is in her heart. It has nothing to do with her childhood home, it can never again be cured by running to her parents.

*

Hestia, at ten, is different from Ilona and infinitely less appealing. Nobody calls her Hestia, but always Hetty, so at least she is not troubled, at that stage, by her lack of resemblance to a Greek goddess. Later she learns with relief that of all the pantheon Hestia is the most matronly, and thinks she might not, after all, be so far off the mark. At six Hetty is stick-thin, at ten she has become stolid; by twelve she will be slim again and at fourteen will fall for the rest of her life into the endless fat-thin cycle common to most women in the overfed Western world. She is shapely but solid, not light.

Hetty is sent to camp, a church camp. She has made strenuous efforts to resist being sent, but these have been ignored, and she is packed off notwithstanding her various medicaments, all to be taken three times a day. From among her parents' infinite network of churchpeople, someone has been found who happens to be going up the motorway in the right direction, three days into the camp week, and by arrangement Hetty is handed over by this person, with a suitcase which will not snap shut, on a motorway lay-by, to someone else she doesn't know, who delivers her right to her dormitory and then disappears.

The camp takes place in an empty boarding school. Everyone else is there in families, or couples; there are a few stray adult singles, but no solitary children. People assume that Hetty belongs to the house-staff, and has thus acquired the right to eat at the camp table, to take part in the prayer meetings. Hetty does these things dutifully and otherwise keeps to herself, reading on her bunk for most of each day, or in the garden. She has allowed one paperback per day in her knapsack, two if one or both is Enid Blyton. When, tardily, one of the young mothers, coming upon her sitting neatly on a garden seat, asks her how she is, Hetty folds her arms across her chest and announces that she is homesick. She senses that this accurate self-diagnosis does not go down very well, that more sympathy would have been forthcoming if she had cried, that it can be better not to know what is the matter.

*

As an adult, Hestia has always been driven by a totally irrational impulse: go home, go home, go home. She goes through this drama time and again, but it always ends the same. Like suicide, a corollary of suicide. Creeping off before the end, bowing out, taking leave. Something is being evaded. Or, like sex, thinks Hestia. Never, ever let yourself go... Her flights are not escapades, but the very opposite: there is no escape from herself, locked in her bower of bone where bliss cannot enter.

What is it that is hidden, what is it that haunts her when she is vulnerable and alone in strange places, that she can't face? Why does she, Hestia, who believes in taking charge of her life, however much she dislikes such tired women's-magazine phrases, suffer time and again this utter desertion of energy and will?

It has always been so. If anything it gets worse with age. Home sickness, like the legacy of radiation sickness, bred in the bone... Those abortive attempts to get away, those mad homing-pigeon escapades... She is sick, she must be, to act like this, a grown woman, what made her sick?

Home did. And if this intuition is true, then what to do with it?

Homesickness has been my whole life, thinks Hestia. At the centre of it. You might even say that life is for defining homesickness in.

*

In Paris, once, in the Café Cluny, a Corsican had explained to Hestia that when you looked at mainland France from his home, near Calvi, and thought you saw Nice, what you were looking at was not Nice but a mirage of it, a reflection, only, somehow suspended in the Mediterranean ether. Replace Nice with Life, thinks Hestia, and this is how she feels, as if there is some unavailable reality, hidden by an illusion of the real. As if it were all a question of getting through the opalescent curtain before which she finds herself tremulously living, to the reality behind it, in which, only, she can be truly alive. And writing, and shrinkage, and the rest, are so many attempts to hail a ship to take you through the rainbow, to where you once where you cannot help believing you once were, and where you can be, truly.

*

There had been a story they told within the church, at their oddly claustrophobic family Sunday lunches, everybody firmly buttoned-up, parochial jokes only admitted.

A tramp had been bothering them for some time. The huge, strangely utilitarian double-doors were left open during the service, to allow for latecomers, and possible Guidance. While it was allowable that the tramp in question had been Guided, it seemed unlikely, for he would shuffle up to the gallery, apparently to be near the heater, and only made impatient grunts when offered a New International Bible, open at the right page, to follow the sermon and understand the relevance of the hymns. This was tolerated for some weeks, but the climax came when a young man, too young to know any better, passed him the offering bag, and a captive audience saw it relieved of several notes from middling to large denominations. And not a plate, but a pouch, a bag, designed for the discreet stuffing-in of tithes by cheque, postdated if need be: so it was quite flagrant.

The next time the tramp turned up for morning service, he did not repeat this trick, but asked for money directly, stopping one of the elders at the door as the congregation filed out. He had, he said, to get to London, urgently. The fare was more than forty pounds. His coat smelt of garbage, his breath smelt worse. So the elder called his deputy, a deacon only but with a tolerably firm handshake, to stand at the door, and drove the tramp down to the station. Afterwards he would recount, with great pride, as if this were the punchline, that he had himself bought the tramp a ticket and seen him onto the train, non-stop to Euston. So he had gone to London, although the fact that he only wanted the money for beer and cigarettes and a few burgers to get through the week seemed to have escaped nobody.

Well I bet that showed him, thinks Hestia wryly, years later, addressing herself to the fading imprint of the actors of this story. She wonders if he saw foxes from the train window, and what London was like when he got there, and cannot imagine that it could have been very hospitable. How did he acquire the money to get back? Or didn't he care where he was?

*

All her life, Hestia will dream of this church. She dreams of hell-fire burning on the horizon of the playing-fields as she sleeps at home; later, of standing in the car-park, next door to the church, and the building collapsing in on itself, behind her. She thinks, with nostalgia, of summer evenings, herself as a small girl in a frilled cotton dress, of the peculiar peace of watching the dust floating in its rainbow tunnel from the austere stained-glass windows, as the pastor preached way over her head...

She dreams of the end of the world, of sitting at a desk as the sky caves in and the moon turns slowly to blood and the last trump is her own scream waking her as she cries, 'Give me more time, more time!' With more time, she could assure her salvation, but never in the present.

'And are you a Christian too, dear?' asks the religious education teacher at school, going round the class: Christian, Sikh, Hindu, Hindu, Christian. And Hetty starts, blushes, mumbles, 'Not yet.'

Salvation postponed. Indefinitely.

*

Being plunged into solitude, thinks Hestia now, winging her random way to Canada, paradoxically detracts from your independence. You lose at a stroke the ability to fall back on your own resources. Like a tourist with a repertoire of endlessly permutable completeable phrases: could you tell me the way to the bank/the swimming pool/the maternity ward? Where can I buy a loaf/a straw hat/a house? Would you be so kind as to repair my heels/my back tyre/my life?

What is a life made of, Hestia wonders, what is her life made of, what is a life supposed to be made of? Is she strong enough, once again, to face tearing up by the roots a whole existence, the explosion of the self into a million tiny pieces? It always starts off so well, is the new place not marvellous, what museums, what monuments, what cafés; you live like a tourist or like a nineteenth century adventuress of reduced means, and then one day it hits you, the unaskeable question can no longer be held at bay: What am I doing here? With shifting emphasis, What am I *doing* here? What am *I* doing here? Life should not be made up of separable chunks, a few years here, a few years there, with nothing to attach you anywhere, nothing to stop you floating off like a helium balloon come adrift: they say, there's nothing to keep you here; and this is freedom...

By the time she goes to Canada, Hestia thinks she has had the worst of her homesick crisis. Whatever does it matter where anyone goes? Be. Get a life. You map out the city in which you find yourself, as a cat maps its new territory, maps and memorises. Or like building your own personal underground system, she thinks, and naming the stops; thus linking the public and the private, the inner and the outer domains; thus slowly making sense of the city, spinning yourself safely into your own web. Making something to keep you there, a network to hold you, with its own logic and contradictions. Making no-place into some-place, over there into right here. Thus in Strasbourg a certain line had begun as a shuttle only, between Hestia's flat and the University, and with the years new stations had been added: the Pourquoi Pas, Lacan, Clinique, Canada House, Acropolis, chez Patrick... for, respectively, the barge where she had had the party after defending her thesis, her shrink's consulting rooms, the hospital where she had been taken after severing an artery, the homes of Canadian friends, Greek friends, and her Sunday-afternoon cake-shop.

One surely should be able to do this anywhere, at random, if one can do it at all. Life as lego. In pieces, separable, *secable*. Nothing to do with each other in the essence, but up to you to put them together? Like dominoes...

But there is this: to be bumped into in the street, to have someone call your name as you go by, or just the possibility of this happening, to make phone calls all around the city for one reason or another, invitations to drinks, books to order, speakers to invite, Hello, this is Hetty, this is Hestia May, this is Dr. May calling, and to be known, to be recognised. You can kid yourself, you can go out and see and do everything, send postcards home to prove it, have, ostensibly, a ball; but it is when you lie down to sleep on bleak Sunday afternoons that you curl into pain, into a bruise, in which all your inadequacies filter into consciousness, through various shades of purple. Hestia has become conscious at these times of an invisible cord pulling her back, in space, in time. *Maman. Maman. Ne me quittes pas, maman.*

Although she is almost certain it is she who left.

Homesickness: try to make a life, yes, thinks Hestia; but I haven't got the pieces...

*

Working for a time in a strange town at the bleak dead period before the run-up to Christmas, Hestia had once been confronted from a bus, stalled at a junction in the blank-windowed dark, with a neon sign which read, between rotating adverts, '*Si tu ne sais pas où tu vas, n'oublies pas d'où tu viens*'. If you don't know where you're going, don't forget where you come from. This had struck her as a proverb torn from its native soil and made to mean something other than was originally intended, but it nonetheless stayed with her, just as surely as once, as a sixth former going for university interviews, the strains of 'Do you know....where you're going to?' piped over the tannoy among the mess of coffee rings and polystyrene cups on Birmingham New Street station had struck home as essential, as profound, and had never gone away.

This, then, is the story of Hestia, of where she came from and where it was she went, and it can only be told by means of the fantasies that grew in the dark of the furthest corner of her mind.

*

She is twelve years old and sitting on the station platform of the town here she lives, when she experiences for the first time a disconcerting intuition which will be with her always.

You could go anywhere, not only go, but you could stay anywhere. So long as you had enough money for your ticket, there was nothing whatsoever to prevent you from packing a small suitcase and catching any train at all. You could stay in a boarding house, paying by the week with the money you would get from the DHSS, then in time you would get a job... What enthralls her is this inexorable progress: not simply the acquisition of material benefits, but of another life entirely. Not a new identity, but the idea that in a wholly anonymous city, one might conceivably manage to function without one.

Yet surely existence is inextricably bound up with the familiarity of home, her parents, the piano, the guinea pigs, ballet after school, swimming on Saturdays, her sisters. Surely one is placed, one does not choose. There has to be something to prevent you from making such a transfer, some control, a limit to where one's own effrontery can take one.

But what if after all growing up were to be only a matter of

95

adding on, at random? Then all that she had become up to that point could be broken off, bit by bit, and she has felt so safe and real, assimilated, accumulated. If this town, on the down platform of whose gum-riddled grime-raddled Victorian station she now stands, can define her, then any town can, any house, any people.

But she is only twelve. You can't claim social security until you are at least sixteen, or get a job. She couldn't do it, it's just a fantasy, a ridiculous fancy in the guise of something real and practical. Nobody would expect her to do it. It isn't even possible.

*

'Do you know... where you're going to?' That is a question without an answer, or much of one, but here is an answer without a question: Hestia, as a teenager, replying rudely to some habitual and irritating remark of her mother's, along the lines of her filial ingratitude for her existence: 'Well if I wasn't here, I wouldn't miss myself.' This has to be, this must be, every teenager's conversation with the parent who screams at one point or another for compensation for the life she has milked out with no reward...

And now she has found out what it is, to miss oneself.

Songs heard on stations. When she had left for France, the song in her head, perhaps absorbed unconsciously from the radio in the furore of packing, had been, *'Aint no sunshine when she's gone.'* It had played, unstoppably, in her head, not just all through that journey, by train and ship with a collection of bulging inadequate cases and carrier bags added at the last minute, but also in every remembered version of that journey. *'Aint no sunshine when she's gone...'.* What is wrong with this, she realises years later, is where she is in the song: not it's object but it's subject. Here, and missing herself, which is no longer there, so must be nowhere.

*

The sewing scissors. The breadknife. The marmalade jar on the kitchen windowsill. Household objects, winging their way through time and ontological space, into memory, into dreams, into this fiction, now. Recuperated objects. Memory as inventory...

Once Hestia dreams of a sideplate with a design of regularly broken concentric circles under a cheap glaze, black on white. There was only one plate of this sort and it was placed under a potted plant. She had never remembered noticing it but she dreamt of it, far enough into her exile to know she was never going home.

*

Later, navigation becomes the key to survival, or to abortion, as in, mission abort, mission abort. In order to feel secure she has to have a certain knowledge, in any given circumstances, of how to get from A to B to C and, most importantly, back to A. She will develop a taste for lodging near stations, and a habit of listing taxi numbers wherever she goes, in case. A few years into her teens, she would have known exactly how to find her way out of that church camp, how to make a run for it, taxi, bus, train, taxi, and there she would be, on her own doorstep, take it or leave it. ('What are you doing here?'... The doorstep is not really her own; out of phase, she is unwelcome as the next door cat's pee in the morning).

Adulthood gives you the right to do these things, and the wherewithal. Hestia has run away from a job as an au pair in Spain, has handed back a plane ticket for the south of France ten minutes before departure and taken her reimbursement of seventy per cent without a murmur, has disembarked from planes five minutes after boarding them, yes, more than once – get me out of here while that door's still open – provoking, on one occasion, a bomb-search and the wrath of Air France. She has walked back through Heathrow the way which in theory you should never be able to come; abort, abort... Similarly, she once moved into a flat in Strasbourg, installed moveables and a telephone, and then couldn't face it, so moved right out again, single-handed, with all her clothes and books and furniture, at four in the morning. This was a story that Hestia would tell against herself, sometimes, when the subject of moving house came up, the likelihood of her ever having participated in these events seeming gradually less likely as she settled down, and as Ilona grew older.

It happened when she had been in Strasbourg about a year, and had found herself having to move into another flat, the one she rented having been requisitioned by its owner, who by law had a right to do so. Hestia had looked over about a dozen, the frankly sordid, the gracious but unaffordable, before settling on a two-roomed apartment in a little squat house some three hundred years old, timbered, beamed, and looking over a small square. The flat was small, but light, and pretty, and well-heated, with a fitted kitchen. Her previous flat having been furnished, she set about buying improvised furniture with her very modest salary, none of it entirely practical or comfortable: baskets to put clothes in, folding chairs, sheet metal shelf units that proved unstable, a single mattress, albeit well sprung, and a plain pine bedstead. She sent out change of address cards to friends and all the usual institutions, had a phone line installed. It was July, the heat and humidity and pollution unbearable, so she waited until after dark to start the move, and made, on foot, a dozen journeys, carting her belongings, until she suddenly changed her mind and began to drag them back again.

Sleeping a night on her new mattress among the new furniture was all it would have taken to bond with her new home, and she knew this – one shower, one nocturnal trip to the bathroom, making one pot of coffee on the stove. But suddenly none of this was possible, and so with the sweat pouring off her, arms and legs shaking with effort, she began to ferry her stuff the other way. Once she got back to the original flat, she knew she was being ridiculous, splashed her face and neck under the cold tap, pulled herself together, and began again to transport – the distance on foot was about half a mile – what she had taken over a few hours previously and then brought back. After that, it was impossible to enumerate the number of times she changed her mind and switched direction, but it got to the stage where the very sight of the new apartment made her want to scream, where for sheer exhaustion and frustration with herself she no longer cared about her possessions or the deposit or the installation fee for the phone, and so she took all the furniture down from the new flat and left it in the scrubby square below. In the middle of the square a young tree was growing, and she arranged her things around it as if it were a standard lamp. Only the little bed-settee was too much for her, so she left it till last and then got it end-on, intending to bump and slide it down the staircase. Unfortunately it stuck fast, and irrevocably, at a bend – so she scrambled over it, let herself out of the front door and into the square for the last time, and sat down on one of her own chairs for a rest.

Her outdoor sitting-room looked welcoming, if surreal, under a lopsided moon, with a teapot on the folding café table, like something by Buchholz; and she stayed for a while until, damp with perspiration, she grew cold. Then, leaving the furniture where it was, she went home to bed, and a week later moved one floor down into the flat directly below the one she had originally been renting, and still managed to feel homesick, especially as she now had no furniture.

With experience she became more adept at appearing to lay the blame for these incidents on other people. She had let it be understood without actually saying so that there had been some insuperable problem with the flat. She had extricated herself from the Heathrow debacle in such a way as to be awarded compensation. After Italy Hestia had steadfastly refused 'to talk about it', and it seemed to have become tacitly accepted that something had happened to her, something sexual, something bad, something worth throwing up your whole summer for and running for home.

And after each of these abdications, what she felt was so predictable that the various stages could be itemised: flooding relief at having got herself out of where she was; encroaching suffocation, at finding herself back where she had started. Despair. This would give rise to the concomitant fantasy, somehow necessary to this syndrome and a vital part of it: to take off, on a plane or a train in the night, long distance, with only a handbag, a toothbrush, a book, and nothing else but a credit card; just to go and be, somewhere else...

*

Hetty, when she was old enough to have a Saturday job in a shop, came home after her shift one day and told her mother that Melanie's mother had died. Melanie was another shop assistant, West Indian, working in the toy department while Hestia manned the Pick and Mix. She must have been about fifteen. 'What will she do?' asked little Hetty, who was now so much bigger.

'Oh, those West Indian families – there'll be all sorts of aunts and cousins around to help her out with the cooking and the housework. It's not as if she was a baby.'

But cooking and housework were not really what Hetty had in mind.

*

For too long, Hetty's little-girl attachment to her mother continues to be visceral, long after the journey down the crimson channel of birth. When crossed as a small child, she would fight against her mother, hit at her belly, and the struggle was to return to pre-birth, to non-being, to somersault back into the protective prison of the womb.

All her life she fears the dislocation and fragmentation of what holds her in place in the universe. She fears ringing and ringing, far away in time and space, and the telephone echoing in an empty house, causing nothing but faint vibrations in the dust. Oh, what have I done? screams Hestia into the void. An ambiguous cry, containing ignorance, or horror.

Ilona

XII

One of the reasons why Daniel initially takes Ilona to Ste-Marie is that, not even intending to bring her back or not quite believing that he would, he has provided absolutely nothing for her in the Nice flat, not a poster, not a bright quilt cover, not a girls' book. By taking her elsewhere, he disguises this fact: he hadn't intended her to come to Ste-Marie, not, he hadn't intended her to come at all.

He is preoccupied, in the first days and weeks, with trying to make up for what seems to him now an extraordinary meanness, an unforgivable desire to impose privation. He buys her drawing blocks and the superior versions of colouring books she favours, with tiny intricate patterns, which, coloured rightly, will give 3-D effects; he buys videos and books of puzzles in Italian, which she is now keen to learn, paints and stencils and sets of pencils with parakeets and palm trees on them. But her room in the Nice flat has to be equipped, properly. He has told her, disingenuously or not, that he wanted to get to know her before doing anything to the room, so that she could choose the furniture for herself. The walls, like all the walls in that square and gracious flat, are white, the French windows, giving onto a little iron balcony, generous; the ceilings are high, the doors double.

The very subject of the flat has been difficult to bring up. Daniel has explained in Canada that he lives between the two places, although term-time, he anticipates now, will tie him to Nice. He has got into the habit, as Dr Echs has suggested, of taking her up to the flat, building up progressively, first showing her round, introducing her to Camilla the cat, then making tea there, then staying the night. They have by this time begun to collect things for her room, but as she doesn't yet have a bed, she sleeps with him in his. Daniel knows by now that she couldn't have been persuaded to do otherwise anyway, the first nights in a new flat. Not even his presence wholly reassures her. There are other demons.

Ilona finds her bed not when they are looking for it, but in a *brocante* in the small town in the south where they stop for breakfast on the way back from the trip to Paris. They both halt suddenly as they pass the shop window, each separately arrested by the sight of a pair of girls' ice skates, perhaps a hundred years old, in cream leather cracked into softness, posed as if negligently on a green velvet footstool. Then Ilona looks past them into the interior gloom, as if she has at last spotted just what she has been looking for.

This is not a bed like other beds. The base is fashionably low-slung, creating an illusion of the contemporary, but banks of arcane and elaborate wrought iron, into which, if one looks closely, are twisted thorns and roses, decorate each corner, rising steeply, and continue almost along the length of the mattress, with a break in the middle, making getting in and out of bed possible. This bed suggests endless luxurious curlings into velvet sleep, it is redolent of a secret inner world; it brings to mind a magic carpet, wafting its occupant into unimaginable dreams. It somehow manages to conjure up an infinitely rich and private inner experience. But that is not all. As time unravels and the subject begins to bother him more, Daniel realises that Ilona's wrought-iron curlicues have nothing to do with decoration. She has chosen protection. Or, possibly, a cage.

The *brocanteur* receives them royally, emerging from the dusty and hybrid gloom to pour tea from a samovar, bringing out whole series of yellow-glazed cups and saucers for their inspection, talking endlessly about his stock, and talking himself, finally, into knocking five hundred francs off his exorbitant price. Ilona sits in the break in the ironwork on the edge of the bed, which she has already made hers, although Daniel has been firm about refusing the goose-feather quilt and ticking mattress, which the brocanteur drags across the shop to adorn a lesser bedstead. When the delivery papers are signed and they are leaving, they both remember the skates. Seated on an old kitchen chair, covetous with her eyes half-shut and enjoying the attention, Ilona is fitted like Cinderella, and the fit is perfect. True, the leather is cracking in places and far from clean, true the laces are so ancient that they snap when pulled, but the blades are sharp and strong, and Ilona will have her ball cleaning the boots up, buffing and shining, making the cream creamy and the silver silver, rethreading the eyelets. They will go skating once or twice before she grows out of them, she in a metallic skating-skirt, and then the boots will sit in the hall in Nice, at the foot of the curly hatstand, and Ilona will decide one day to thread them with old lace, dyed emerald, or crimson, or purple.

*

Life in the Nice flat is not always simple. One Saturday afternoon, Daniel is working in his study, happy with his work, at one level perfectly peaceful, brain buzzing furiously at another. Ilona comes in, trailing round the half-open door, and asks if she can make a pie; in fact, a cherry and almond tart. She likes baking, is good at it, this very fragile little girl, and is somehow grown-up when she is doing it, making the minimum amount of mess, generating only necessary washing-up and putting the kitchen to rights while whatever it is is in the oven. Cooking is one thing, eating is not so simple.

Daniel asks if she has finished her homework, which she has, so he says yes, and no more is heard from the kitchen for some time. When he starts to smell the baking almonds, Daniel goes to see her, and finds her sitting on her bed behind the wrought-iron scrollery, reading; she doesn't look up when he comes in.

'Did you make your pie?' he says, and she tells him, still with her eyes on her book, 'It's a horrible pie.'

He can see something is wrong, so he goes into the kitchen and checks on the pie, opening the oven door minimally. It is slightly risen, beginning to be golden, the pastry perfectly evenly trimmed around the edges. He cannot imagine why she should call it a horrible pie, but when he goes back into her bedroom he sees that the reason she isn't looking up is because she has the beginnings of tears in her eyes. He sits on the edge of the bed, always a little awkward as the ironwork makes Ilona difficult to reach, takes her arm and shakes it a little – she is stiff – and asks what's wrong.

And his gaze holds her, and she can't resist him, and hating herself for giving in, she says, 'I thought you were going to help me.'

'What, with the pie?' Daniel knows he hadn't even thought of it, that he just hadn't wanted to be interrupted, had been on a curve that brooked no interference. He tries to tell her this, to be honest, but he also says that he is sorry, that if he'd realised she wanted him to help he would have done, they would have done it later.

He remembers a cross-channel ferry, Caen to Portsmouth, towards the end of a long crossing, five hours. There is intermittent drizzle outside, it isn't fine enough to go out on deck, or not for very long. The passengers have now been herded together in the lounges for more than four hours, watching the uninterrupted greyness through the portholes, sky and sea almost undifferentiated, picking their way to the bar over each other's untidy piles of baggage and the excrescences of folded baby-buggies. Sitting among all this there is a child who does not seem to belong to anyone, a girl, slightly too old and not quite sufficiently appealing to be called a little girl: blonde, stocky, freckled, probably about eleven. She is apparently captivated by the toddler belonging to the family camped on the row of seats opposite. His name seems to be be Callum, but she calls Cal-man, Cal-man, over and over, trying to make him come to her, trying to take him, struggling, onto her lap. When the mother comes to the rescue, to dismiss and reclaim, she wants to know how old he is, what his second name is, where they have been on holiday, where they live.

The questions go on and on, the girl seems to feel a sort of desperation, not to let the contact drop. After a while this begins visibly to grate on the mother's nerves, courteous as she is at first; she packs up their things and at the very first signal they move down to the hold, leaving a noticeable silence behind them. The girl sits on her hands, looking after them, resentment plain on her face. She looks as if she knows she has been irritating. Then a few minutes later an extended broadsheet dismantles itself opposite her, and from behind it there emerges a man in a sports jacket, and with a dried-up face, whom hitherto the paper had completely screened. 'Come on,' he says gruffly, his only recorded words, and the girl gets up without looking at him and begins to follow, keeping a yard or two behind. Her father.

*

'My stomach hurts,' says Ilona later that evening, reluctantly in bed, and Daniel accepts this, doesn't try to persuade her out of it, massages her skin lightly, asks if that's better, kisses her cheek and tells her he is there, just in the next room.

105

'I'll tell you a story, he says, a story about –'

Corin. Corin had been a boy of fourteen or so. Twice seven, off the dice, which now sit in a little japanned bowl on the high shelf Daniel has fixed up above and along Ilona's bed. Daniel cannot remember where he got this story from, but thinks that he didn't read it, that somebody told it to him, and that that somebody might have been Hestia. Ilona may have heard it before. Anyway, he has started now.

Corin was a young boy who sometimes got into trouble. Well, pretty often, actually. He used to steal from Woolworths, petty stuff, sweets and records, presumably for the attention, and he swore at his mother a lot. Yes, this must have been a flip of Hestia's narrative dice, the family were very low-church and couldn't take this, it was sin. Hestia's own family he has always imagined in hats and dark coats and at loggerheads, like Munchmen. It had been less like living on an iceberg, she had told him once, than conducting a civil war on one; and he had recognised this pronouncement as considered and final and filed it away for reference. He does not encumber the narrative with this.

Anyway, for Corin things went on and got worse (in the manner of violently disintegrating and dislocating families – he doesn't put this in either). He was very rude and very badly-behaved, but in fact when he went to his room at night he was glad to be warm and safe in that house with his adopted parents and brothers and sisters. There were several of the latter.

Corin was the only one who was adopted, and there was some mystery about his origins. He was good-looking in a slight, sharp-boned sort of way, but much nicer to look at than his pasty, lumpy siblings, and as time went on his skin grew observably darker.

Silver identity bracelets were the thing then, and he used to wear one which was blank. He had asked his adopted parents frequently who he was, where he came from, but they didn't want to tell him. A lot of the fights involved this question.

To make things more complicated, there had been at the church, Daniel recalls Hestia had said, a very beautiful young girl of a similar age who looked just like him and like nobody else in that town, but his name had been Corin Brown and hers had been Nina Smith. So there couldn't have been anything in it, or so the respective adoptive parents liked to say, or not to say, because saying it would have been like admitting something. Daniel misses this bit out, too.

So things got more and more agitated in Corin's house, and one morning he screamed at his mother as usual over breakfast, and then went off to school. Just before lunchbreak, he was called out of class. It was geometry (Daniel puts this in for Ilona, who dislikes the subject), and they were having a test, so he was pleased to skip it. Corin had to go and see the headmistress, and he was puzzled, because in general he worked hard at school and did well, and the policeman had said the matter of the shoplifting wouldn't be taken any further. But it was this that pricked at his conscience nonetheless, as he knocked on the door.

When he walked in, he was surprised to see, standing right in the middle of the carpet, a suitcase. He was even more surprised to recognise it as one of those dusty old cardboard trunks with the ridged plastic handles belonging to his parents and hauled out once a year, for the holiday on the Isle of Wight. Then he knew what was coming.

The headmistress coughed and looked at him. 'Er...Your mother – ah – came to see me this morning. Sit down, Corin.'

Corin sat down. And the headmistress found herself obliged to break the news that his parents had decided to disown him. This was not the word she used, but it came to the same thing. He would not be going home that night but would be taken to a hostel. Before the afternoon was out, Corin, who had not said anything to his friends about what had come to pass in the headmistress's office, was called in again, this time to meet his social worker, a thin, unhealthy-looking young man who gave him his benefit book and his new address. Five, Acacia Road. His parents lived at number eleven of the same street, but nobody remarked upon this.

That evening Corin took his usual bus and got off at his usual stop, to ring on a different doorbell, and to be met by the house mother, a dark, broad, pleasant lady in her early forties, whose name was Consuelo, and whom Corin had maybe seen around. She showed him where the tea things were and said, 'Never mind. We have a good time here. There's only me and the five of you, you've got your own room. It'll be just like home.' And she showed Corin to his room, the boxroom beside the bathroom, which was in the same place as the one he had had before, in the other house.

This story, or the telling of it now, is designed to comfort, to reassure, like gloating on little girls, or boys, left in the paths of big bad wolves in the forest as you sit warm and safe before the fire. Or even wicked stepmothers and real good mothers, suddenly resurrected; you could interpret it that way. He remembers too late that Ilona can't take horror stories, even those with happy endings, even in a well-lit room, that she cries and has bad dreams. She takes everything in the first degree, so that what he had intended as the moral of the story has to be spelt out to her: Don't worry, I'm here, rock-a-bye-baby, I've got you and I won't let you slip from my grasp, won't let you down, you're safe with me... Is he not there at the school gate or within it at five o'clock every day? Has he not caught this child hurtling through space and screaming for the loss of her mother and given her love and a home and a rosy wrought-iron bed and a jointed eight-inch teddy-bear?

Several days later, *à propos* of nothing, Ilona suddenly says to Daniel, 'It was worse for Corin because he was adopted. They said they'd chosen him and that they would never give him back and then they did.'

This is Hestia's version of adoption as explained to Ilona when she started school.

*

Corin was visited several times at the hostel by the unhealthy-looking young man and after a while, started to go up to London with him on a Sunday, instead of going to church. There he met a lot of people, none of them very healthy-looking, and was given money to let them take his photograph, wearing a towel around his hips or nothing, more often nothing; so he didn't have to steal any more. Daniel doesn't include this part of the story because he doesn't know it, and even Hestia never knew the end.

*

Not the next night, because there are after all nights when Daniel is not in, and others of TV or reading before bedtime, Ilona tells.

At Ilona's school in Canada, when she was eight or nine, one child had been absent for a week, and came back looking pale and pinched and hollow-eyed. Sister Ignatia had come into their formroom to tell them that Jennifer's mother had died, and that they must all be very kind to her, more than usually so. She was a popular girl and there was no need really to ask them to be kind.

Perhaps it was this that made Jenny bow her head with a sudden jerk, like shame, not actually crying but somehow worse, so that Sister Ignatia asked for someone to take her for a walk around the playing field until the end of the period, which was biology. Ilona was making a diagram of the stomach, full and empty, showing the action of the valves. Nobody volunteered; even Jennifer's best friends, Nadine and Julia, were trying to look as if they hadn't heard.

Here Ilona's fragment of narrative ends. The rest is not yet ready for formulation. In the end, Sister Ignatia had taken Jenny herself, and Ilona had kept her head down and gone on colouring in as her friend crossed the classroom, stumbling a little as she went and blushing. All the girls felt ashamed, and knew they hadn't been able to want to go because Jennifer's mother was dead and they were going home to theirs at four o'clock and so there was really nothing to be said. It must be the worst thing, Ilona had thought at the time, clenching her fists under the table, the very worst thing of all. This she remembers, but does not tell.

*

In the absence of stories, reading is something Ilona does curled right up at the head of her bed on a pile of pillows, almost out of sight behind the dense tracery of the ironwork. When she is upset or ill or just has to be persuaded to go to sleep, Daniel will read to her, Hestia's own children's books, which have been sent over, *The Borrowers*, which bears real reading, *The Wolves of Willoughby Chase*; Noel Streatfield and Rumer Godden. Ilona is an eclectic reader, and her material includes piles of British school stories, Enid Blyton in the original versions, before they got made politically correct, with their tales of exclusive establishments where common girls are resented and tins of pineapple consumed at midnight are the highlight of the term; Elinor M Brent-Dyer, whose extraordinarily high moral tone does not seem to bother Ilona; stories of more modern and liberated girls at a luxury establishment in Cornwall, where boyfriends are allowed and the girls wear make-up and go out at weekends. Daniel marvels that she should show such interest in the fictive antics of a tiny social class in a country she has never visited, although perhaps she feels it brings her closer to her mother. Hestia had in fact attended ordinary state day-schools except for two tense and bewildering years in the sixth form of a prestigious boy's public school, where, being unceasingly bullied, she had taken refuge in the library, emerging emotionally shattered but extremely accomplished – although even the library had not been free from schoolboy flashers and mooners. The incongruity of the memory of Hestia telling him this makes Daniel smile when he sees Ilona reading about the prim existence of Britain's little pre-war heroines. It amazes him that she, so individualistic, will throw herself with such enthusiasm into the world of these establishments, with their almost military discipline, the brutal machinery of ticking off and bringing down a peg or two. The books she likes best are more complex, the characters more rounded: the Nicola Marlow books avoid or circumvent the repeat-frame, as predictable as pornography, of first day, half term, end of term; there is a real world of interesting relationships and disharmonious home life and, occasionally, financial problems.

Daniel wonders whether Ilona dreams of having her trunk packed by a maid, having a hideous uniform with a felt hat and a tie and blouses that button up the back bought for her in Harrods, and bagging a corner seat as she departs Paddington with the Fenellas and the Jaynes and the hockey sticks for half a term in a dormitory, with only flimsy cubey curtains for protection and Matey for emotional support. This needy little girl who can't settle down for one night without him – does she have a private yen to strike out alone?

XIII

Taken for the first time to see the brand-new, angular glass and concrete buildings of her new school in Nice, having refused point-blank to discuss the matter all summer (Dr Echs has said to leave it, that she'll come to it when she is ready), Ilona gives a start backwards at the gate and digs her nails sharply into Daniel's hand, reminding him of a cat he had tried some years previously to transplant from one flat to another, and its reaction – clawing and clinging and spitting all at the same time – when he had shown it the new garden. When asked about this reaction to the building, she had implied that it was the physicality of it that put her off, what she read as its bleak hostility. Dr Echs had provoked a thoughtful silence by suggesting to her that this focusing on her fear of new and strange buildings was perhaps a way of avoiding the more difficult question of her relationships with the people inside.

Daniel has organised a pre-term interview, a visit around the empty school. They are received in the special unit to which Ilona is to be attached, designed for children who for one reason or another have difficulty fitting into the mainstream, the foreign, the gifted, those with adaptation difficulties – into which category Ilona has found her way, given the piquancy of her medical reports and what he has succeeded in presenting as her brutal uprooting from her native land. The persistence of her antipathy towards school seems to be, thinks Daniel, yet another manifestation of her regressive-dependent streak. Besides, her school in Canada, which he now knows all about, was a small and intimate establishment with girls only, where Ilona had been in the penultimate year. But it is not essentially the size of the other pupils which puts Ilona off, or the presence of boys, it is the prospect of daily and prolonged separation from Daniel. At the interview she hides behind him entirely, answering all questions in a monotone as if she resents so gross an intrusion into her privacy, as if only Daniel has the right to speak to her.

The special unit, which is in a much older and more welcoming rosy stone building, part of the private boarding wing, has all sorts of facilities meant to help the children settle in: they each have their own desk to start off from and go back to, there is a sick room where they can lie down and to which they can adjourn if it all gets too much, and a room where they can speak to a counsellor, albeit on a certain morning, from eight to ten, in alternate weeks.

Daniel, who has felt desperate for space, knows he will have difficulty leaving her here. He can picture Ilona, cornered in this would-be cosy room with its posters and magazines, rebuffing all means of eliciting information and fantasising herself back into her little world of Daniel, Dr Echs, and the few other privileged beings allowed in: Sabine, who comes to be with her when Daniel cannot, Brigitte, an acquaintance of Daniel's who has recently become a friend, and whose daughter, Catherine, is not only the same age as Ilona, but appears, so far, to look sympathetically on her erratic temperament. He knows, too, that Ilona feels outrage: not only does she not want to leave him, she feels that if he loved her, he wouldn't let her leave.

Back in the Nice flat, once school has become real and is to be faced less than two weeks away, Ilona becomes restless and unsettled. She proclaims and perhaps even feels enthusiasm for shopping trips with Sabine in search of text books, stationery, clothes and shoes, and spends a long time in her bedroom unwrapping and arranging these objects, trying on the new outfits, as if in quest of some elusive adequation between herself and the new version of that self which these accoutrements require. Daniel encourages them to buy Cacherel notebooks and Snoopy set-squares, anything that will make the alien environment feel more like home. It is on one of these shopping trips that they have the idea of the telephone. Windowsfull of 'packs' are arranged in brightly coloured pyramids, sold as another back-to-school gimmick. Consulted, Daniel at once sees the point – one of these gadgets as a sort of substitute maternal breast, or ear – but will not be seduced into picking one up with the pencil cases. He writes down a serious list of their requirements and takes Ilona to a good shop, where she is equipped with a quality instrument, which nonetheless can be provided, and is, to please her, with a set of clip-on covers, either in pastel shades or primary colours. She agonises over this for some time while Daniel fills in the paperwork, but finally takes the primary.

*

Ilona's impossible behaviour starts a few weeks after the move to Nice, when Daniel, officially, stops letting her sleep in his bed. The habit, slipped into from the beginning, against all advice, against all good sense, has been difficult to break. As he says once to Dr Echs, if you know you can calm a wildly screaming, hitting, biting Ilona by agreeing to take her into your bed at night – where she will cuddle against one, warm and endearing, all thought of revolt over now that she has got her own way – then how can you not do it?

The alternative is whole evenings expended on calming her tears and imprecations, and sometimes for sheer exhaustion, for the need of quiet, he will anyway give in. And when this has worked once she knows it will again. Dr Echs has suggested rationing the time she is allowed in Daniel's bed, letting her in sometimes for breakfast on weekend mornings, and said that if she does come in at night, there should be only a brief stay on the understanding that she then goes back to her own bed, even if he has to take her there and settle her down all over again.

Ilona's trump card is that she never has nightmares when she is in Daniel's bed. This is true, but when Dr. Echs asks her what then they can conclude from this, she isn't yet ready to tell him.

*

A difficult phase sets in, like bad weather.

One stormy day, at a time when Daniel and Ilona are locked into a protracted conflict, she, by more or less having a tantrum, manages to stay home from school in the morning, giving Daniel an elongated day; he can get practically nothing done before noon – sporadic phone calls, trying to look through a file, interrupted by having to deal with Ilona, having to get her lunch. Now he will end up getting into the office about two, and so having to stay till ten, which he could do without, and he had wanted to go to the gym, and now won't be able to get it in; this annoys him, he can feel his muscles itching, and perhaps not only his muscles. He gets her to school by coercion, by telling her he doesn't give a damn if she cries, that she'll find herself there, shortly, crying or not, so she'd better make an effort to pull herself together. He makes her a *tisane*, brusquely, packs up the cold lunch she hasn't eaten for her to take with her.

Ilona is indeed trying to pull herself together, according to her lights, because she cannot, possibly, go out feeling so raw, so unprotected. She pulls on her outside self with her jacket, and sits sipping her herbal tea, waiting for him, waiting to be told what to do next. In the car, neither of them says much at all. When he drops her off, she pulls away from his kiss, because she can't afford to do otherwise at this moment, slams the car door and doesn't look back; she doesn't see him drive on a few yards, and pull in, and sit nonetheless watching her, unable to bring himself to abandon her so summarily. She slips inside the gates, pauses, props one foot on the block of concrete that holds it open, looking down, deciding what to do. Then she glances back, fails to see him still there, and puts her fists up for a moment to her downturned eyes. She looks to him as lost as a two-year-old in a crowd, when any other child her age, he thinks, with a stab of irritation and tenderness, would have gone on, resolute, just to show him. He shoots out of his seat, slams the car door harder than she did, and sprints over to where she stands.

'Lili.' He contemplates her through the rust-coloured bars of the high gate, and she looks back with that lucid pained-angel stare of hers. He hesitates, unsure now what to say next. 'Sabine will pick you up tonight.' This she knows. 'Try and have a good day, pussycat, hm?'

She nods, saying nothing and not approaching, but she is near enough to the bars for him to reach in and squeeze her half-turned shoulder through her jacket, and then they both walk away without looking at each other again.

*

Some nights, Ilona will get to a stage where she is beyond tears, beyond resistance, and will let Daniel do what he likes with her, becoming a doll, passive, to be undressed, bathed, put to bed. Yet when he gets back that evening, she resists, standing in the bath with her t-shirt still on, folding her arms feebly across her stomach as he goes to pull it up over her head. He pulls harder, she, already exhausted, gives in, and lets her arms fly upwards, exposing as she does so a dried trickle of brownish blood on her stomach. Her navel, he sees, is red and bleeding and ragged and crusting; she must have been picking at it incessantly. She winces when he runs the shower over her, and doesn't say a word when, having dried her off, he fills the little hollow with antiseptic cream and smoothes a large square plaster over it.

*

'What is somatisation,' says Dr Echs when Daniel mentions this, 'but expressing oneself through the body? And by scratching at her navel until it bleeds, until it becomes infected, what is she expressing, about the bond with the mother?'

'Which mother?' says Daniel. 'Do you mean Hestia, or me as mother?'

'It isn't a question of what *I* mean.' Dr Echs replies, as so often, without answering.

Dr Echs has always courteously but firmly insisted that he has to treat them both if at all, and the following evening, as every Friday, Daniel takes Ilona to her session and sees the doctor afterwards. Today Daniel agrees that Ilona is restless, inclined to be sleepless, disturbed by the whole business of going to school, of being away, unprotected, all day. She comes into his study at night, when she is supposed to be asleep, and wants to sit on his lap, which he lets her do for a little, typing or scrolling through his text with his left hand, his right clasped around her waist. 'I can't sleep... I don't want to sleep on my own.'

'You remember what we said?'

Patiently, Daniel had gone through it again the previous evening. When she is in bed, he is a mere few yards away, she can leave her door open and the hall light on, he is not about to leave, and anyway, even when he is not physically with her, he is with her inwardly. She had stilled in his arms as he pronounced all this, as if one more repetition was all that was necessary. In her room he had smoothed the sheets and pillows, plumped up the quilt, dropped his voice to a whisper and talked her into sleep.

'But around four she woke up; I had to change her sheets.'

Dr Echs says, 'Why is it that you use that euphemism? Does the subject embarrass you?'

Daniel says that it does not. That perhaps he is trying to spare

Ilona's dignity, to protect her. Who is it, asks Dr Echs, that he is trying to protect? And Daniel thinks, without being able to prevent it, of his silent ride back to boarding school in the train, through the snow, to collect that missing report. That same holiday it had happened to him more than once. His father had wanted to beat him, but his mother had protested that he had caught a cold on the kidneys during his needless journey, and thus the hostilities had shifted from his sphere to between his parents, out of his orbit.

*

In Daniel's bed, nevertheless, a few nights later, Ilona applies her lips blindly, vainly hungry, to his nipples. This arid activity demands at least the cessation of her screaming. Her flooding tears have drenched the planes and hollows of his chest, it is the slick of her own grief that she licks up and the pathos of this produces more tears, more desperate sucking. She will not go back to her own bed, and he refuses, at one in the morning, to enter into a round of the hysterical crying and struggling that any show of firmness in this issue tends to induce. In this area at least, firmness does not seem to be what Ilona requires, although she wants it in other situations, and from other people. Dr. Echs orders her on those occasions when she flings out of the room in anger or embarrassment to come back, sit down, lean back, stop that, take deep breaths, stop crying, and she subsides immediately, feels, it seems, a primitive pleasure and propriety in this filial obedience.

But Daniel is beginning to take account of Ilona's limitations, for his own protection and practical well-being as well as hers, and sleeping alone in her room without Daniel has recently become again, on many nights, one of them; even if from her own room he is visible in lamplight, just through an open door. So she screams and claws for her own way and lies once more sobbing helplessly in his arms, her back to him, arms weakly flailing, letting him grip her around her waist and across her chest, her fragile haunches pressed against his crotch through the pyjama bottoms which he now feels obliged to affect. She is appallingly needy, appallingly ashamed.

Coerced back into her own bed, sheets will inevitably be wet. Dr Echs has said that washing her face and hands with cold water is not altogether a bad idea, that they can try gently to train her body out of it, but that where it goes on is in the mind, which will not be forced.

She tells Dr Echs on one of her difficult, truculent days, 'I don't see how telling you things is going to make me stop'.

'Stop what?'

She interprets this as mildly sadistic because he knows that she always has difficulty getting the phrase out, will willingly let herself be led back to it, a co-operative if turbulent child, but, so far, never in so many words. She says, 'At night.' He looks at her with the beginnings of his patient, radiant smile.

'Do you want to stop?'

She is caught utterly off guard and sits on her footstool, knees to her chin, looking up at him in astonishment.

'Think about it,' he tells her, 'For next time.'

*

Ilona takes these injunctions absolutely literally, and begins the next session as if no interval of time had elapsed at all, as if the flow of their communication or communion had not been severed and no other activity had supervened on either side. She says, looking at the carpet, screwing up her courage, 'Sometimes it's nice.'

He says nothing and she steals a glance up at him. He has managed, notwithstanding this supreme piece of obliqueness, to re-engage, and she sees this and carries on. 'Daniel comes. He stays with me and tells me stories about when he was little. When I have bad dreams.' She feels frustration because she cannot tell him too about the perverse pleasure of the warm flood itself, and knows she is not getting to the root of things.

Dr Echs, who has heard from Daniel about Ilona's nocturnal tempests, concludes that the peaceful scenes she evokes, with the man soothing the child back to sleep, her trust, his love, uncomplicated, must take place on other nights. 'If I didn't do — that,' she hazards, 'he might not come.' The air vibrates with an unspoken question mark.

'Exactly,' says Dr Echs, enthusiastic. 'Very good. Is that how it was with your mother? Mamma would come in, sit with you, stroke

117

your hair, you didn't have to be on your own all night? Lost in the dark?'

And Ilona's grief, tamed over time, is suddenly once more a hairsbreadth away. Her face dissolves into wetness, sobs bubbling and tearing as she gathers momentum. It is rare that he physically touches a patient, but he touches Ilona more often than most; now he half-guides, half-lifts her from the footstool and settles her in the velvet chair, brings a box of tissues, crouches in front of her, although she cannot see him for tears, and tells her to get it out, to let go, taking her hot hand, peeling the strands of soaked hair back from her cheeks.

*

In the end, for want of choice, Ilona gives in, reluctantly, to the routine of school. By indicating, falsely, that he may well take his ward back to Canada the following year, Daniel has won for her a specially tailored timetable, involving a great many periods of private study for correspondence courses and individual supervision, and the minimum possible amount of time spent with her class.

Ilona doesn't fit in at school and doesn't see why she should try. She keeps herself to herself, passing near to those she frequents without interacting with them, like a fastidious cat. She makes an exception of Catherine, spending break-times with her and sometimes with her friends, sitting on the steps of the annexe, largely out of sight of the masses.

By pleading fragile health, he has got her a truncated day, so that she can spend more time at home. Dr Echs's consulting rooms are an easy walk from the school, Catherine is never far away, and Ilona has her telephone in her school bag: there is thus a whole network of escape routes and emergency exits. When he can, Daniel meets her at lunchtime and takes her to a café for a sandwich or a salad, or, her favourite, tartines. On Friday afternoons he picks her up and goes with her to see Dr Echs, to wash the week away, Ilona says. Dr Echs laughs at this, but sees the point.

The weeks pass in the Nice flat, from late summer to the following spring. Ilona has music on Wednesdays, tap-dancing on Friday afternoons; on Saturdays Brigitte often comes over with

Catherine, or else they go out in the car. Catherine sometimes comes after school and stays the night, and on other days they giggle together on the phone, or lie on her bed in earnest counsel. Daniel is pleased to see that their friendship is beginning to work both ways. When Catherine's father, who left Brigitte and lives in Corsica, tries to lure his daughter to his new home with the promise of all-day riding lessons, recognised and refused by Brigitte as a way of having her without looking after her, and amounting to buying her off, Ilona puts her thin arm around her friend's shoulders and sits with her in silence.

Ilona's eleventh birthday comes and goes. Daniel takes her to choose a necklace at a good jewellers, but she wants a bracelet, inside which something can be inscribed: her name, the date, with love. He buys her a tiny heart-shaped pendant as well, and fastens it around her fragile neck, stopping to marvel at the pale, silky underneath hair when she lifts up the rest. Later she watches, wide-eyed, as he lights a camp fire in a stony *calanque* and cooks sausages; she tells him later that she had always imagined a father, doing that.

The consultations with Dr Echs continue, sometimes in long, serene curves, but not infrequently with tears and blacknesses and fits of despair, which, incredibly, resolve themselves into smiles and sighs of relief and periods of serenity, and, Daniel supposes, growth, otherwise there is no point. When Ilona is ill, once for a week with flu, Sabine comes to act as sick-nurse, and Ilona has a bed on the settee, or sits on the floor doing her jigsaw map of the world on the coffee table, depending on the stage of convalescence she has reached. At these times she will demand Daniel's attention as soon as he comes in the door, bringing with him magazines and exotic fruit-juices, and love and concern in an almost palpable aura. Richard comes for the weekend several times, and, at Christmas, they go back to Paris to visit him.

Daniel battles to establish a routine, to work, fighting to prolong the uninterrupted periods in his study. The time he spends at the office, once cut back, has never quite re-established itself, and he tries to clear space in the evenings. In theory, Ilona is in bed by nine, but there are evenings still when she cannot or will not settle down, when she will come into his study and want to sit on his lap, to

119

be fussed over and cuddled, and sometimes he still lets her do this.

And at the same time, Ilona learns to manage Daniel's moods. Even, occasionally, it occurs to him that she might be humouring him.

*

Throughout the flat, ashtrays and pintrays and the bottoms of fruit-bowls accumulate little deposits; ribbons from small gifts, to and from Ilona, with pieces of wrapping paper still stuck to them, little gold hairgrips with coloured butterflies or birds on the end, stumps of pastel crayons and odd gold sleeper earrings. Two pairs of tap shoes, crimson patent and white canvas, take their place in an alcove in the hall, next to the cream kid skates.

Daniel sometimes wonders whether he has woken, like Silas Marner, from the trance into which he fell after David's death. Before that he had never given up hoping for his return.

*

Once when they get back to the Nice flat after a Sunday out, a good day, what Ilona calls a holiday-in-a-day, with Brigitte and Catherine, Ilona looks at the clock and suddenly realises she has missed her weekly comedy, her soap, her contact with the delicious artificial world of father, butler, nanny, secretary, three children and the nanny's extended family. Daniel is put out at this, exasperated, and tells her he had thought they'd had a nice day, that she is never satisfied. And that there's a whole stack of back-copies of it, if she's that bothered, in among the unlabelled videos, from the Wednesday evening repeats when she has her dance class and they programme the machine, if they remember. To his surprise, this actually cheers her up; she rootles through the pile, slots one in, settles herself into a corner of the sofa, which is vast and enveloping in a wholly different way from the sterile vastness of Lily's settees – and is apparently perfectly happy, taking her *tisane* from him in sleepy contentment when he brings it in, running her fingers over the velvet beneath her. And he realises she wasn't, in fact, being awkward, that she just needed her ritual, that, on Sunday evenings, this inane emission is something she relies on. He thinks how very uncomplicated, paradoxically, are some of her requirements.

Later that evening, Ilona, in her pyjamas, white cambric with pink embroidered daisies, half lies, still peaceful, on the sofa, in a provisional sort of way, like a cat afraid to settle in a forbidden place, waiting to be told to go to bed. Daniel comes in and fulfils this parental office, switching off the television, sending her off to the bathroom, switching on the lamps in her room and turning down her quilt. When she comes out, he swings her up into his arms, caught for a second with a quick love for her cleanness, her slender fragility, and they stand like that in front of the clear new mirror looking at themselves, her thin legs wrapped around his hips. Daniel sees that there is no irony in her gaze; this is the first degree. He puts a hand up to touch her hair, which is now thicker, longer and blonder from the sun, flicks at it, making it swing, and she smiles at him in the glass, letting him do this, making no reciprocal move, her filial prerogative. For a moment he holds her tightly, then deposits her in the soft receiving envelope behind the black iron roses, and all in this movement her arms unfold themselves from his neck, and she has fallen gently and immediately into sleep.

Daniel is learning to deal with her, but in his head persists the inexplicable image: Ilona is a child in 5/4. Complex Ilona, unique Ilona; there will never be another child like her.

*

In the early hours, one morning, after a night out, when Sabine has slept over in the study to keep Ilona company – the word babysit does not come into their domestic vocabulary – Daniel lets himself in, exhausted, disgusted, sick at heart. He steps from the shadowy hall into the moonwash that mosaics her floor – she never closes her shutters, to sleep – and sinks into the wicker chair by her bed, which does not fail to creak. Ilona sleeps on, smiling a little in her dream, foetally curled, with her back to him and with an old silk scarf peeping out from under the quilt, relic of the Canadian existence.

Afterwards – after any of these times – he can never get away fast enough. If he sits here and watches her sleep, her innocence will emanate. The stolen dummy has slipped from her hand and lies by her cheek on the pillow. He has never openly mentioned the dummy to her, leaving it around her private possessions as she leaves his condoms around his, unquestioning. When she turns over to face him, partly waking, he replaces it between her lips, and she makes a surprised little sound, like Camilla the cat, when you stroke her in her sleep, sighs, and slips back into her dreams.

When his hand stretches out to bestow the habitual caress on her cheek before leaving, he finds himself drawing it back. He cannot directly touch her. But he likes to think of her here in his absence, curled and dreaming, with Camilla, immobile, eyes open in slits, at the end of her bed, facing forward, like the monument at the prow of Ilona's dream-ship, or a familiar hitching a ride into wonderland.

*

Not everything is easy for Ilona to understand. Once, on a weekend morning, she comes into his bed, burrowing into him, as she does, seeking heat and flesh, to claim the affection which is her due, and which he is happy to bestow, except that he has a morning erection, and she asks, for the first time, what it is, hard against her slender thigh.

'I just need to pee,' says Daniel, gets up and does so, and then calls, coming back from the bathroom, 'Right, sweetie, are you going to get up now and get going,' and doesn't come back to bed. Ilona lies in the middle of it, full of emptiness and longing, unsure whether to feel chastised.

When is it that, for the first time, her hand, very sleepy, finds its way down between his thighs and stays there, and he, with just the first stirrings of an erection, doesn't move it, but lets himself drift like that into dreams?

XIV

In the late autumn following Ilona's adoption, Daniel finds himself required to go to Paris with a colleague to join Max, to entertain Japanese clients, the aim being, after the exchange of due courtesies, to establish a contract. Daniel has arranged for Sabine to come and be with Ilona for the weekend, but on the Friday in question, when Daniel comes home, with forty-five minutes to spare before his flight checks in, and Ilona, back from her tap dancing class, is supposed to be settling into her weekend without him, she suddenly explodes with grief and refuses to countenance his going away: in a fit of blind unreason, which will not be contained or placated, she goes on screaming, no, no, NO! As time moves on, Daniel tries all his techniques: the negotiator, the empathiser, the disciplinarian, calm-but-firm, without making the slightest impression on her wild despair. So he makes a snap decision and tells her he will take her, and springs into action, throwing things for her into his bag while phoning Max, who, exasperated but trying not to appear so, takes on the business of contacting the airline for an extra seat. Sabine is encouraging all concerned to sip camomile tea.

By the time the taxi comes, Ilona is partially, but only partially, recovered; she has stopped howling but is in a fragile state, a state of shock, tears still coursing down her cheeks. Daniel sits, on the way to the airport, holding her head against his shoulder and talking business over her head; he has given her rescue remedy to calm her down, but he knows what she really needs to calm her: physical contact, the soothing of skin, of flesh, the stroking of the hair. Driving to the airport reminds him, in between listening to his colleague talk, of the journey to Canada to go and collect Ilona for the first time, and he feels an ache of something almost unbearable; feels this in the midst of this outrageous long-term inconvenience and of the total unacceptability of her current behaviour, as he contemplates this warm, living child, who weeps still because she couldn't bear the thought of being parted from him for three days. His arm tightens around her. He can feel her heartbeat slowing, back to normal.

Daniel has to go and sort out the tickets as the matter concerns his daughter, or ward, so Ilona goes off with the colleague to look at the things in the window of the not very large airport shop. He, kindly, goes and dampens a wad of kleenex under a water fountain and presses it to her hot face, tells her to take a few deep breaths. He wonders fleetingly what it must be like, a lone man with an eleven-year-old girl who springs from nowhere; you can't even do the basics, take her into the washroom, say, to tidy her up properly, and there's nobody else to do it, nobody female...

Max, meanwhile, Daniel discovers – Max who has a great and clumsy affection for Daniel, and by extension (or perhaps not only) for Ilona – has had the brainwave of relocating the whole weekend away from a hotel, faceless, anonymous, in the centre of Paris, to his own house, near St-Maur, outside the city, almost sufficiently far outside to feel like the countryside, *la douce France*. Hilary, his wife – sad, gaunt, a recovering alcoholic – has, Max says she says, enough in her to produce a five-star meal for a few visitors at the drop of a hat, and has already been busy with the daily help and a neighbour, partly to dazzle Max, Daniel imagines, for he has long stopped loving her but still admires her. In this way, the Ilona-factor can be accommodated; Hilary, Max assures Daniel, will be there, Hilary will pull it all together.

All three of them – Daniel, the colleagues and Ilona – feel a whoosh of relief when the plane takes off and they are safely on the way. Ilona risks, 'Are you angry?' – and Daniel says, no, just a little hassled. And that once a decision is made there is no need for anger or recrimination. But that she will have to understand that he will barely be able to see her over the weekend, that they are here to make an impression, not just to get a contract, that there will be a great deal of eating and drinking that she won't be part of, and a great deal of talking that she wouldn't even want to be part of. That when they arrive, it will be straight from the plane to Max's chauffeured car, an hour's drive, and then, straight to the kitchen for her or to bed. That the following day they have a visit to a site, and so he won't see much of her then either. She says, simply, 'Okay,' but he can tell by the way she says it that she's taken it in, that the rules are established. He strokes her silky hair against the flawless cheek and feels her heavy, dreamy. But she suddenly says,

'Will Sabine be lonely?' He says he doesn't know, that she might. And Ilona doesn't answer.

Arrival is a little fraught; Max, at the door, ruffles Ilona's hair and hustles the men, and after a very cursory wash and brush-up, they disappear into the oak-panelled dining-room in a waft of importance and determined conviviality. Hilary takes Ilona upstairs and then down to the kitchen, where the women have a party of their own going, and are rising to the occasion admirably, determinedly. An extraordinarily complex dessert, a pyramid of choux pastry and cream, has been delivered from some distance away, and the delivery-girl is giving very precise instructions about how to cut it. The room is warm and full of excitement, the hors d'oeuvre are about to go out – fantastic creations with sea-creatures appearing to crawl over and from them. Hilary sits Ilona down at an unoccupied corner of the table and gives her soup, knowing that she doesn't want to be in the kitchen to eat but because that's where the people are. But she eats nonetheless, and gets drawn into the general excitement, and polishes glasses and coffee spoons, while Hilary goes off to serve and clear, each time with an air of extreme irony and defiance.

When she can get away for a little, Hilary sees Ilona up to bed, which is one side of the bed prepared for Daniel. Some time after two he comes up, almost drops onto the mattress, reaches for her where she lies in the corner, pulls her face to his chest, and says, 'I'm glad you came.'

XV

Back in the Nice flat one evening a week or so later, Camilla, curled on Ilona's bed in a demure sort of way, front paws crossed with a surely conscious grace, is absorbed. The lights are off, except for one small lamp, and Ilona, sprawled on the bed behind the cat, is making shadow puppets on the wall, rabbits, mostly, as these are what she does best, wiggling her index fingers for the ears; she can also do two dogs fighting. Camilla, rapt, does not apparently differentiate between shadow-rabbits and insubstantial dogs, but darts her wet nose towards both. The front door clicks when Daniel comes in from work, and Ilona goes immediately to bring him to see, but Daniel has already disappeared into his bedroom, switched the shower on almost before he has put his briefcase down, and when Ilona returns to her bed, Camilla gets up and yawns, arches her back superbly, and slinks away. As soon as Daniel is out of the shower and dressed, Ilona stands hanging onto the door of the salon by both handles, swinging and bending backwards, in a way that annoys Daniel, not because of the forward thrust of her small pelvis or the cascade of her blonde hair behind, but because he thinks she will pull the handles loose from the door, which shouldn't really matter, as no real damage is likely to be done and he is not short of screwdrivers: he is annoyed, nevertheless, at the prospect of an evening with no respite after a day of irritations at the office.

'Don't do that', he says, and Ilona, in the same instant, begins, 'Camilla – '.

'What?' says Daniel over his shoulder, striding through to the kitchen. Ilona does not reply; when he comes back she is still hanging on to the door handles, leaning her forehead against the door, crying.

'What's the matter now?' Snappish.

'I was trying to tell you,' she sniffs, 'about the puppets – '

'What puppets?' Dry.

At this, Ilona actually bangs her forehead against the door and says, 'You don't care, I'm not going to tell you now,' and cries harder. She is desperate for him to make some move back towards

126

her, and stands suspended from the door, half inside half out, crying hard.

'Ilona, sometimes you are unbearable,' Daniel tells her, his tone sharpening, and Ilona, because she is not sure what she has done, begins to ask what she has done wrong, in effect to whine, with all the time the weight of what she had wanted to tell him about Camilla dragging on her solar plexus, when it had been something warm and delicious, something saved up to tell him even while it was being carried out.

Daniel is by now really angry, and tells her she is behaving like a baby, and that what she deserves is a slap – not noticing the contradiction – and picks her up, not gently, on his hip, to get her away from hanging onto the door knobs, administering the slap in question along the way. Ilona immediately interprets this as reconciliation, and reaches up to put her arms around his neck and bury her face in him, but he takes her movement for further resistance to his control, shouts at her, 'That's enough,' and deposits her, unceremoniously, on her bed, telling her she can stay there until she has calmed down, shutting the door firmly on his way out.

Ilona lies and sobs at his abominable unfairness, and vows inwardly that she will refuse to come out when he calls her for supper. And even this feeble weapon backfires, for the invitation when it comes is pretty curt anyway.

'If you don't come into the kitchen to eat you're not having it in your room.'

No answer. She stays on her bed on her back, the froggy cold feeling still lodged on her midriff. Tears still shoot intermittently from the outer corners of her eyes into her ears; in the morning she will find little blobs of wax on her pillow....

At what is her official bedtime, Daniel, slumped at his desk trying to go through a file he is too tired to follow, hears her get up and go into the bathroom. He waits a little. When he goes into her she is under her quilt and refuses to speak to him or to respond to his attempt to stroke her hair, which he doesn't do nicely anyway, in Ilona's view; they are both still angry. He hears her crying; she cries herself to sleep.

Next day, they are supposed to be going to join Brigitte and Catherine at Brigitte's sister's house near St-Raphaël. Daniel has slept badly, feeling guilty about Ilona. She doesn't come in to him as she usually does on Sunday mornings, and he realises that his bed, at this particular juncture in the week, feels empty without her. Going into her room he finds her awake; the curtains appear to have gone undrawn. He tells her, neutrally, that she'd better get up if they are to be there on time. A few minutes later, he comes upon her, dressed, at the kitchen table; she has opened a raspberry yoghurt and fetched a spoon, and is now sitting there looking at it, still red-eyed. This annoys him again, and he tells her to just eat it, then says more kindly that if she doesn't want that one, she can put it back and take another flavour, just to cover the open pot with cling-film. His tone, to her ear, is still hostile.

'Answer me when I speak to you.'

But Ilona, who doesn't really know what the question is, says 'Yes' uncertainly, tear-choked again, and he sees that she is not going to eat it and that there is no point having a row over it. He is also determined not to sit down, hold her between his knees, put his arm round her and feed her, as he has done so many times before. And which is what she irritates him so much by wanting.

Once more dangerously impatient, he puts the yoghurt back, tells her to gather some bread and fruit together and put it in a plastic bag to eat on the way.

In the car, with the radio on, Ilona looks out of the window.

Daniel tells her off for fiddling with her seatbelt clasp, asking her, nastily, whether she wants him to get a childproof one, as for a baby, and she stops looking out of the window and looks down, but doesn't, as far as he can hear, cry. He doesn't care what she does.

He says nothing about her breakfast; after a while she reaches for a banana, breaks it in half, and passes the half still in its skin over to him – who doesn't want it – and in taking it back again, she drops it on the floor of the car, and he shouts at her again, and this time she breaks into silent tears punctuated by the odd escaped gasping sob, and lets her own half fall onto the seat. She gives herself up entirely to crying, pushing her fists into her face; in the mirror she looks like a little animal in distress. So he stops the car, very shortly, and gets out, opens her door, clicks the forbidden seatbelt clasp, and picks her up. As soon as she arrives in his arms and he says, 'It's alright, I'm just being a crabby old bastard,' she clings to him and cries louder with relief, with release. She has no idea how to cope with his withdrawals, is radically ill-equipped to cope, but it troubles him that she is so easily bought back.

It begins to rain, a sudden squall, through sunlight, almost over before it has properly begun, and a rainbow forms briefly, bridging the world as far as they can see. As they drive on, a patch of it still hangs against the sunlit grey, raggedly iridescent, surprisingly persistent.

*

Nonetheless, in the end the atmosphere between them provokes a state of emergency in the Nice flat. Unable to work or to sleep, at the mercy of Ilona's sudden and absolute refusals to go to school, Daniel calls Richard in Paris, who comes up with the idea of an exchange. Richard will come down on Thursday evening, Daniel will fly up on the Friday, coming back on Sunday evening. On Monday they will all spend the evening together and Richard will leave on Tuesday. The version that Daniel tells Ilona, who is finally calm in her room after a very rocky day, is that he has to go to Paris on business, but she is sufficiently astute to see through this, looking oddly adult as she contemplates his lie in silence.

'I think we need a little break from each other,' he says, aware of sounding falsely reasonable, and then, more sincerely, that loving someone is something that you do, actively, not something that you simply feel, and that he thinks he'll do it better when he gets back.

She says nothing; she has tears in her eyes, and he wonders how brutal this sort of reasoning must sound to an eleven year old. 'If you really don't want me to,' he finds himself adding, 'I won't go.'

Ilona tries, 'If I'm good... will you still want to go?'

Their eyes meet, and he sees that this is a sort of joke: she doesn't expect him to say no. She is giving her permission: I won't make a fuss, but don't forget I've got a claim on you.

Ilona wants to know if it is Richard who is coming because he is a psychiatrist. Daniel laughs and says that so is Dr Echs. They have a perfectly amicable discussion, Ilona lying with her face half-hidden behind the rosy iron tracery, reminiscent of a baroque nun in a parlour, Daniel leaning forward in the wicker chair, absently caressing the solid black petals. Nonetheless, before settling down to sleep, exhausted now and regressing in her fatigue, Ilona still feels the need to ask, Do you still love me, are you definitely coming back, will you call me to say goodnight... . And having obtained the answers she needs to all these queries, she turns over sweetly, like a child of three, and goes to sleep, thumb in mouth, her blonde hair, by now much longer, trailing over the pillow in lazy points. Daniel fingers a strand of it and marvels at the peace now emanating from her. Asked what had so suddenly calmed her down after her session with Dr Echs, to which she had gone in tears and despair and with no hope of relief, she had said simply, *'Calmement'*. This was apparently what he had said to her, and it had slipped, she said, into her ear and all through her body and right down to her toes. What is it, Daniel wonders, that prevents him from having the same effect?

*

When some days later Daniel tells Dr Echs about this and puts the question to him, Dr. Echs looks pensive and says, as often, that he doesn't have the answer, but that what comes to him immediately is that he, himself, rarely touches her, only listens and talks. Daniel says,

'How can I not touch her? She demands it, she always has. If I didn't I'd probably get the sack from the position of step-father.'

'You're very defensive,' says Dr. Echs.

Daniel, who keeps his distance from the doctor when he can, considers this but makes no reply.

'Are you putting yourself in the position,' asks Dr. Echs, 'of a man who shouldn't be touching an eleven-year-old girl?'

*

Daniel has not loved a man since David died, although his flesh is occasionally stirred, without reference to his mind. Even this ceased altogether for about eighteen months after David died, and he felt himself shrink into himself, as if his genitalia had actually shrivelled a little, retracted. 'Normal', or at least understandable, perhaps, but he wasn't going to go to pay anyone to be told so. He imagined, grimly, that this was what aversion therapy must have been like, the sort of thing that his father would have liked to have done to him, if ever he had known, or been able to accept the knowledge that must, after all, have lurked. Right, son, lie down and think very hard about that guy on the tube, the graceful narrowness of his hips, the little piece of bared tanned flesh exposed at the waist where his shirt has pulled up over his belt, the fact that he was certainly giving you the eye. And here it comes, wham, the electric shock into your brain making your flesh go cold and limp, making your skin crawl, contracting your throat and bringing tears to your eyes.

Daniel had had to take photos of David's body, before he, or it, was brought out of the cave. At least, he had presumed this would be necessary, and he didn't want anyone else doing it. He had brought a precision camera for this grim purpose, before leaving London, in case the need should arise, and it had now arisen. Dr. Allen's corpse, viewed from the mouth of the cave, from two feet to the east, then close up to show the peculiar twist to the neck. The film had been black and white, but every time he looks at these photos, Daniel sees screaming slashes of red. When he has been with men, picked up at the gym, in cafés – nice guys, all of them, successful, funny, good-looking – these slashes have come back in orgasm, and the image of David's mouth, open, in pain, dying, and he, Daniel, not there to save him.

In reality there had been very little blood, and what there was was weeks dried, congealed.

And now to have David's smooth hard flank, David's smile on waking up next to him, most lost mornings, and his other hardness, replaced by this insignificant female child? This is to be milked dry, this is a denial of any attempt at love and life and freedom. Intolerable, blood-leeching claustration. And yet, Daniel knows although he tries to hide from knowing, it was over with David, long before he was killed. Once, in the summer dusk in the attic of the Balham house, Daniel had seen, on the screen of his mind, superimposed on the sweep of the lawn down to the railway line, a candle, burned down to nothing, about to flicker out. He had known what it meant, and had ignored it, but it was an image which, afterwards, would come back to ridicule him, to mock, in particular, his stealthy, ever-inventive, ever-thwarted plans for getting David back. It had been a time of self-doubt – am I sufficiently clever, sufficiently beautiful, sufficiently lovable, and if so why should he have left? Therefore I can't be... Daniel had put everything into a social life designed to make him once more worthy; mirrors and lovers and gossip told him that he was beautiful and clever, but David had left anyway. Daniel had made a show, a show convincing even to himself, of adapting the upstairs flat for solo habitation, shifting furniture and emptying wardrobes into suitcases which disappeared on David's discreet daytime visits when Daniel was at work, but he had kept traces of David around. Photos of the two of them together hung now on the insides of alcoves, surfaces invisible when you walked into the room, or had been removed from their frames and stacked as if casually on the bureau in a heap, ostensibly waiting to be sorted out, but in fact never moved.

It turned out that there was someone else involved, and had been for some months. Thinking about it later, Daniel knew that for David he had already long been a candle which had burnt out. For some time – how long? – there had been no reciprocal flicker in his lover's eyes, and Daniel, who had always had trouble with affairs of the body only, had, as their bed was invaded figuratively and sometimes literally by beautiful third parties, withdrawn into solitude, curling in on his loss, his pain. It had been summer and he had lain on a chaise-longue among Yan's carefully luxuriant Dutch borders, with the cats, in silence, not reading, soaking up heat and pain, at the end of resistance and before knowledge. Resentment and a bleak hatred had come later. This was hardest to believe when he had discovered David's senseless body in its cave, when a thousand small cruelties and public rebuffs had risen up like a flock of ruffled birds and left forever. Daniel remembers searching for the one spark that could perhaps have re-ignited life, if he had arrived sooner, if the record of wrongs in his mind had not prevented him from setting out for the airport the moment he was visited by the first apprehension; or if he had not already immolated himself in resentment, set hard like molten rock, before David had disappeared.

Afterwards there had been guilt, as if David had had to die in order to get Daniel off his back, to force him to leave him alone. Yet paradoxically Daniel is sure, in a faraway corner of his mind, that David would rather be alive in his, Daniel's, smothering arms, than dead and alone and nothing.

Daniel passes on this story for a long time. He finally tells Ilona a version of it one night when she is warm and heavy beside him in bed in the Nice flat, settling down for sleep. She receives it, gravely and without comment. He reflects later that she is probably one of the few people who understands, not the extent of this loss, but the nature of it. Or perhaps he offers it as an attempt to balance her pain.

*

Even after the break with Richard, the cycle goes round, essentially unbroken, and trouble flares intermittently.

'Are you still angry with me?' Ilona emerges now with her cat-like shadow-tread into the door-frame of the study, unsure, for there has been more shouting, more mutual incomprehension.

Daniel, at his desk, looks up at her sharply, and says, 'A little, yes.'

'I don't know what I've done.' Supplicating, not defiant. She is learning to manage his moods, but solitude and an overwhelming need for the confirmation of his affection have driven her out of her room, where she has been curled on her bed, not crying but feeling slapped and hurt, shrivelled and small, to seek his company.

'I told you what you'd done, and it's not the first time.'

With all her eleven-year-old goodwill, Ilona does not know how to take this: as dismissal or a signal that further penitence is required and thus further questioning on her part. She says nothing, and Daniel makes a concession to her youth that he certainly wouldn't have made to an equal, and goes through it again. 'If I speak to you, you answer me, that's all there is to it. You can say you don't know, I don't expect you to know everything, I don't even expect you always to feel like talking, to me or to anyone else, but the least of things is to acknowledge me when I speak to you.'

'I thought I did,' said Ilona, who knows she did, but knows also not to make this statement, naked and unattenuated.

'You mutter and speak too quietly and I lose my patience. You can speak clearly enough when you want to.'

Ilona feels vaguely that there are some things you don't say straight out but which need rehearsal and concerned solicitation, but she cannot formulate this, and has learnt not to lash out at him without being sure of her defence.

'It's a lack of respect, Ilona. I think we can do better than that, and I think you can do better that that.'

She still says nothing, remembering the summer, when they first came to Ste-Marie; then she was not expected to speak. They had existed for days, perhaps even, intermittently, weeks, within the limitless spaces of her silence. Now she senses that not to speak, once more, is dangerous.

'Sorry.'

'It's easy to say sorry. It has to go in, here.' He reaches out, half rises and taps her gently on the temple, and she stands, still awkward, unsure whether this is a signal that requires in answer her approach as he sits down again. But Daniel is indeed still angry, with everything and thus with her, the nearest available object, and he says, cruel, 'Go and do your homework, hm?'

A little later, when he calls her for dinner, without having asked her to come and help, which she usually likes to do, and without, he now remembers, having taken in her glass of orange juice as he generally does when he is home after school, he sees that she has been crying, again, and that she has not dared ignore his call or keep him waiting.

'Alright, pussycat?' he says, and she replies with a 'Yes' of unnatural clarity, when normally in this state she would have nodded and looked down. A tear splashes onto the cloth beside her plate. The gratin isn't yet brown, it can wait; still half-annoyed, with her and by her existence, he pulls her roughly onto his lap and says, a command, 'Stop crying,' which makes her cry more, silently, soaking the shoulder of his shirt.

'What do I h-have to do?' she raises her head to say.

'Do?'

'To stop you – h-hating me – '

'Oh, Ilona, my Lili, my little dandelion.' He expels a long sigh and with it his animosity, and sits patting her slender little hip, gently, rhythmically. 'You can't, possibly, imagine that I hate you.

Who wipes your tears, hm?' He catches one with his tongue and turns it into a kiss on one cheekbone. 'Who reads to you when you're in bed, who phones you every break-time when you're at school, who takes you to Forest Hill?' Who changes your sheets at night, he might have added. She is crying harder, and he rocks her, wordlessly. He knows she knows, that not 'knowing' that he loves her is a defence against what he might do to her next, and he finds her need and her vulnerability and her total dependence on him insupportable. 'I couldn't love you more,' he tells her, truly, 'if you'd come out of my own — belly — ' He hitches his shirt up and reveals his navel, at which she laughs, the creasing of her cheeks sending a suspended tear careering into the dry little crater, where it lands, hot and surprising, and into which Ilona immediately dives to rescue it with the tip of her tongue, tit for tat, grinning up at him from his lap with her eyelashes still wet and her lips, which she bites when she cries, very red; not arch, he realises, simply full of delight at her own joke. When the phone rings, he stretches across the table and picks it up with one hand, flipping her onto her stomach across his lap and casually smacking her bottom with the other, then clamping his elbow across her waist so that she cannot escape. She lies, wriggling and giggling into his crotch.

'Yes, Max,' says Daniel. 'OK. OK, just not now.'

XVI

It is like being inside a tent with the rain beating down, when someone puts up an irrepressible finger to trace the fall of a rivulet on the canvas, breaking the tension, letting the deluge in. It happens next day, when Daniel tells Ilona he has to go away.

She sits at the table, opposite him, in the kitchen, very markedly not eating, and says, 'I'm hungry.' He says, or does not say, Do you want me to feed you? And he goes round to her side of the table, and spoons mashed potato into her mouth. It is impossible to be angry with her when he sees how she accepts the food from the spoon, but it is all too possible to hate her. Daniel produces calendars and lays out maps on the parquet in the sitting-room, to show her where he will be, and when, which is a very long way away, in the Far East, for a relatively long time. Ilona will not look, covers her ears and burrows into her corner of the sofa, legs curling automatically into the foetal position. This pathos pushes Daniel finally not into pity but into an explosion of righteous indignation; he is taking the time to explain to her, he points out, not everyone would do that, he is trying to make it easy for her. At this Ilona unwinds from the settee, leaps up and is in one movement in her room with the door slammed violently behind her. But within seconds she is back, and in her hand is the little mobile phone he bought her, and what she does is hurl it across the room towards the mirror over the table, where it sketches a lopsided daisy of cracks into the bottom right-hand corner of that vast and elegant glass, itself falling almost gently to the parquet, and bouncing apart into two chunks.

Daniel's arm grips her waist before he can stop himself, in what might have been the beginning of an embrace, but turns into a violent shove; she lands spread forward over the arm of his chair, shocked into stillness, and he picks her up roughly and carries her through to her room, intending to put her on her bed and leave her there. In the time it takes to cross the room she begins to weep hysterically, and he is furious to feel her small bottom wet against his shirt. She is screaming, 'I hate you!', and trying to thrash against him, struggling to free her arms.

Truly angry, fighting to contain her, he tells her in a voice of steel that this may well be, but that his patience is finite, that he will not tolerate this sort of behaviour, that she cannot count on him to put up with this right down the line, that he will not stand for her behaving like a two-year-old at the age of eleven, that she is going to have to learn to behave in a more pleasant way and one more appropriate to her age. When, he shouts in exasperation, is she planning to stop this nonsense, at eleven, at twelve, at thirteen? He swerves away from her bedroom as she continues to struggle, and more or less drags her into the bathroom, holding her disgustedly away from him, pulling her t-shirt off over her head, not gently; he hauls her jeans and pants down, and takes advantage of this to smack her, hard, in passing. This makes her cry in a different way, immobile with her hands to her face as she stands naked in her inadequate thinness, which irritates him even more. He pulls his own now damp shirt off, then dumps her brutally in the bath and turns on the shower.

His swing misjudges, he uses too much force, she slips and falls, snagging against something in her fall, and lies in the bottom of the bath somehow crumpled on one side with her back to him, her left arm twisted under her. Her crying has turned into something Daniel recognises, appalled, as a roar of terror and pain. Blood is coming from somewhere, a great deal of blood. It takes Daniel a few seconds to work out that she has gashed her wrist on the metal soapdish which is set into the wall, and against which he must inadvertently have made her slice her arm in her fall, trying to save herself from him. He is stunned for a moment into shifting quasi-comically from foot to foot, he cannot leave Ilona to get himself to the phone in the hall.

The doorbell rings, which forces him to act; it is the Professor from upstairs, who has heard the noise and wants to know if there is anything he can do. Daniel has no choice but to usher him in to the spectacle of his naked child in the empty bath, still twisted over her wound. When Daniel sits her up and turns her over, there is a trail of vomit on her chin and chest, and the beginning of a bump above her right temple. There is blood, too, on her forehead; he must have scratched her with his signet ring as he took her t-shirt off. Her left arm from fingers to forearm is entirely flowing red. The Professor takes this in, and goes into the hall to phone for an ambulance, telling Daniel to take her out of the bath and wrap her up. Daniel is almost afraid she will scream for help if he touches her, that she will give him away, but, wrapped in a bathsheet and then in a blanket, with her damaged arm kept upwards, over his shoulder, soaking his shirt to crimson within seconds, she sobs into him, not against him.

He sits and rocks her and tells her that he's sorry, and the Professor goes through the drawers of unfamiliar little girls' possessions to find what she might need for the hospital.

The ambulance men shine a light into Ilona's eyes and monitor her pulse on the way; she has no idea where she is being taken, through the dark. Her head is spinning, she cannot remember very clearly what has happened. She knows she needs to keep on crying to make sure that she can, and she knows now also that she has a right to do so. Then, aware of feeling sick again, she closes her eyes and takes refuge in silence.

Daniel sits in a side room at the hospital while Ilona's wrist is stitched, thinking about how it feels to be the sort of man who knocks his child about. Not even his child. Even more classic, thinks Daniel, darkly, still horrified, unable to believe what he has shown himself capable of. To lay into a child, and such a helpless and lost child, when she got upset because he was going away. This is what it boils down to, thinks Daniel, as he waits for Ilona's damaged artery and tendons to be repaired. He looks down the years that have led him to this and hates himself, truly.

Later she lies, white but sleepless, in her hospital bed, her hurt arm massively wound round with hot bandages, making a heavy mass which she cannot as yet feel except as a dead weight pressing on her ribcage, across which it has been laid to ease the circulation. There is an absolute lack of rancour in her expression, in the few words she has pronounced. She seems to want him to talk to her, to explain the strange objects around her; she says nothing of what has happened but seems to accept it as natural, inevitable.

She is given an injection to calm her down and soothe the pain, and the nurse tells Daniel she will probably sleep till morning, and that he should go home, get some rest, come back at six if he wants to be there when she is woken up.

Ilona, who feels as if she is floating through the dark in some unknown time and space, thinks, addressing herself to Daniel, You could slap me, punch me, push me downstairs, take a knife and re-open my wound and I would still love you. This she swears. She has not yet learned to feel wonder, or disgust, at herself, or him.

XVII

Dr Echs phones Ilona, not in the hospital but when she gets home to her rosy iron bed, where she stays, weakened by shock and by the loss of blood, which is not serious, Daniel has been told, but will nonetheless take time to make up. Her ragged little wound is still bandaged, though now more neatly, in a hard casing, her hand and wrist sore and stiff from the stitching. It is difficult for her to dress, to wash, even to hold a book and turn the pages. For a few days she sleeps a lot and lets herself be spoilt. Daniel reads to her, plays game with her, makes a little nest for her on the sofa from which she can watch television, trying to work while she rests, which is most of the time. They don't talk about the accident, and Daniel's going away is not mentioned. Cancelling her appointments, Daniel has given Dr.Echs a streamlined version of events, with his own part in the accident for the moment omitted. When the doctor phones, Daniel tries not to listen to Ilona saying that she is feeling better, thank you, and that she is sorry she has not been able to come. He can nonetheless hear in her voice that she is in fact sorry for this; there is a wordless appeal. He knows that her attachment for Dr Echs runs extraordinarily deep; also that in some way it bypasses him.

When, one evening, after an hour or two shut in his study, he finds that Ilona is nowhere in the flat, he is not wholly surprised.

Walking past as if casually Ilona has been almost sure there will be no light showing at Dr. Echs's window from the street, and relief floods through her when there is. The house where he has his office is smiling, entirely symmetrical, the arched front door plum in the middle of the ground floor, with a large brass knocker in its own centre. The building resembles a child's drawing of a house, her own idea of a house when younger. She slips silently up the stairs and sits in the waiting room, until Dr Echs treads down the corridor, opens the door, and regards her in surprise. She is not looking, she does not speak. He takes this in and sits down on one of the cane chairs, perpendicular to her, to wait.

'Daniel's going away,' she tells him, thinly, after some moments.

'I'm listening,' he says, and takes the fingers of her damaged hand, peeping out of the plaster. They sit for some moments in silence, until she sighs, closes her eyes, and nods her consent when he suggests phoning Daniel to tell her where she is. She knows that this is all she can have, that there can be no completeness. It both is and radically is not enough.

*

Daniel's next visit to Dr Echs, several days later, is driven by guilt, and is also urgent and unannounced. He says he is a hopeless father to her, that he hates and resents Ilona when she is being impossible, but then how achingly, hurtingly sweet and beautiful she is when finally she goes, as she always goes, to sleep after a huge scene, wrung out, empty; and does it have to take violence to love her so much? Dr Echs says that on the contrary he thinks Daniel is a good-enough step-father, but he stops him there.

*

After what is referred to as her accident, Ilona is lethargic, passive, but sometimes also melancholy and unreachable. One night a few days afterwards, having helped her to bathe with her bandaged arm sheathed in a plastic bag, Daniel lifts her out of the water, wraps her in a bathsheet and sits her on his lap, where she twists round to face him, pressing his hips between her narrow thighs, her right arm, more softly, around his neck, her split left wrist resting on his shoulder. 'I want to be your baby,' she says into his shirt, and in her head she sees herself telescoping back into his body, a neat ovoid capsule; not even breast-milk is what she wants, although her face is pressed against his chest: she wants, needs, wholly envisages, this much more radical way of being his baby, to be conceived by him. His text, his object.

In the process of her movements, the towel has fallen down, leaving her naked against him, and part of it is caught, rumpled, between the spread of her legs and his erection. Daniel picks her up and carries her on his hip, sits with her in the wicker chair beside her bed, shifts her thighs once more gently apart with the edge of his hand, and begins to stroke softly, with an immensity of tenderness, between her legs.

There is no climax, no violation of her containment. He slows and calms her, lays her on her stomach on her bed and rests his hand, heavy and warm, between her seraphic shoulder-blades. She sleeps, lost within an immense sigh of relief.

This is not sexual, in the accepted sense of the term, for either of them. It is simply inevitable, absolutely right.

Ilona will never forget this. The tentative spread of the thighs, the wetness between, her face burrowing into his jumper, eyes closed, perfect serenity, the birth of the first silent cry of pleasure, choked in the throat. Brand-new, absolutely virgin, the very first time; there never can or will be anything to match this casually monumental ecstasy; utterly unknown, and at the same time, like coming home....

And yet Ilona, curled in bed in the half-dark, knowing Daniel working in another room, consciously secure, is aware at the same time of her own inviolable solitude, her body, her being, limited and delimited under the quilt, sufficient to itself.

Hestia

XVIII

Strasbourg, six months prior to Hestia's departure for London.

Hestia, stuck in a fallow patch, after her doctorate and before anything else, looks out from her apartment into its closed courtyard and grieves for her work, for days spent in libraries, for the quick vibrations of her fine-tuned mind, which even now she can feel slackening, sagging. What is worse, the fact that she no longer has anything on which to focus her intellect is leaving her prey to old ambitions, packed away in storage to make room for the overwhelming imperative of her thesis, and long ignored. Criticism seems to her suddenly hollow, she has said what she wanted to say, and that was the training, only, she now knows, for something larger, far more pressing: she needs to create. Anything else has just been getting in the way.

I lack a language, murmurs Hestia to herself, and thinks fierce thoughts about being made to write the six hundred pages of her thesis in her competent but foreign French, like writing in the dark, she has always said; and now she wants, with all her heart, to recuperate her language: her mother tongue, she thinks savagely, has been taken from her, torn out. She needs a language in which she can make something, not criticise and deconstruct the makings of others.

In the university library, now, Hestia is leafing through Freud, although leafing hardly covers it: this is a deliberate act, twenty-four navy-bound tomes, some with their buckram boards pitted and scratched, ordered up to her place, a neat double pile fast becoming a heap, orderly-disorderly, as she leaves volumes open, inserts markers, lets her space spill over onto the floor. There are a few unsatisfactory references, hinting only at the enlightenment she seeks, red herrings, thinks Hestia: Sexual abstinence; Sexual intercourse, incomplete; Sexual trauma; Sexuality, female... Unpleasure... Vagina... But Freud on vaginismus, as such?

She goes back to the Index, glances through it idly and discovers a gold-mine in the List of Analogies. Barbarian migrations. Dams against flood. Divided loyalty in war. Eruption of lava; Frontier control. Houses moved from one site to another. Intercommunicating channels filled with liquid; Internal haemorrhage. Kinship of mankind and legal kinship. Military mobilisation, River choked by rocks, Robbery on a dark night. Tunnel pierced from two sides. Undesirable guest.

And Hestia-Hesita is sidetracked. The list of analogies makes sense of a kind, or a wonderful web of nonsense; or an anti-web of non-sequitur, refusing to connect and yet, humankind being what it is, setting up faint echoes in the mind, irresistibly stimulating the urge to narrative. It can be read as a poem, strings of signifiers cut loose from signifieds, referentless language. Some of the analogies are wonderfully discursive: Primitive races have had Christianity thrust upon them. Others are poems in themselves: Memory that stinks; Overcoat woven of lies; Six-months' foetus at a ball. Still others could be, should be, pub-names: The Hypnotised Umbrella. Some are quite clearly historical novels: Crassus and the Parthian Queen.

You could make it into a board game, thinks Hestia vaguely, although they would have to be somehow sorted out. They read like crossword clues, so perhaps a sort of scrabble. Or Consequences:-

He was: Turkish gynaecologist
[Fold down]
She was: Housemaid with knowledge of Sanskrit
[Fold down]
They met in: The Mushroom and Myceleum
[Fold down, &c.]
With: Borrowed kettle
He said: Good watch-movement and valuable case
She said: Made in Germany
Then they discussed: Intercommunicating pipes
And the consequence was: Addiction to narcotics

Or:-

He was: Long-sighted rabbi
She was: Traveller singing in the dark

They met in: The Apple Tree and Bean
With: Sounding-board and tuning-fork
He said: Eat or be eaten
She said: Gadarene swine!
Then they discussed: Infinitesimal calculus
And the consequence was: Syphilis

Consequences is a game redolent of childhood, of birthday parties, Christmas day. And yet even at the time, not an innocent game, because it allows for the oddest juxtapositions, encourages juxtapositions to become conjunctions, and then there are connections, which maybe can't be faced.

Consequences, thinks Hestia, is a very pregnant image for how a novel is written, in some sense like dice, another game of chance. In Consequences, you can't see what comes before or what comes next, and when you open out that folded sheet of paper, there is a process of making sense, which may lead to blank incomprehension, or a horrible revelation – or something, perhaps worse, which cannot be understood, but which remains, suggestive, disturbing, dark.

In spite of Prozac, taken in its minty liquid form – a sort of communion, ensuring salvation as the syrup breaks over her tongue – Hestia will wake at night, just on the very edge of sleep, with a gasp, heart speeding, fear scuttling on her skin, with always the same question in her head: What is it that I have forgotten? Some revelation too horrible to be borne, or born? Revelation, Apocalypse, the cutting-off of love.

'It's the only language you understand,' thinks Hestia, suddenly, remembering slaps, and worse, and her pathological shrinking-away.

Polar expedition ill-equipped, murmurs Hestia, thinking of her childhood home, or perhaps of life in general.

Smallholdings on earth and estates in the moon.

XIX

What is young girlhood to a woman? The other side of the coin from what Nabokov flips up in Lolita, or just a change of position, from object to subject? Hestia will lie on her bed in Canada, seven months pregnant, her hands folded across her swollen ripeness with its patterns of silvery scars like the markings on a tabby cat, ankles elevated on cushions, knots of pain in her back, and remember very precisely her young girl's body, her child's body, its neatness and economy so efficient that she inhabited it without reflection, before the split. If there was nymphancy, then she was not aware of it. But there was a sort of secret surety, an unspoilt compactness. The hopeless paradox is that Hestia would have liked, then, to be desired, she now knows, when it is irrecuperably too late.

What is her eleven-year-old self to a woman in maturity, in middle age, as she looks down the long, the aching tunnel away from that time?

Nabokov had it right about silky skin, about translucency, about life as one long irradicable trail of nostalgia for that time: not for sad, sick Humbert, but for the grown-up women he hated. For those women, too, can be eternally in love with pubescence, or of some mythical version of this, and so, forever stranded.

*

Hestia is at the gynaecologist's before the pregnancy, before the rape.

She is going to be told how men react to women, how he reacts to her. 'You don't mind me saying this, do you?' There is real, overpowering embarrassment, her cheeks are hot, but, worse, she is wet between her legs. She feels as if she is being sucked into some vortex of abstruse desire which must surely be reflected on her face, and that she should resist, but she is also egotistically fascinated. What is she like? She is about to be told.

'Men react to women in different ways', he goes on, and the essence of his argument seems to amount to the fact that he perceives her, Hestia, not as a mother, or as a lover, but as a child, with a child's needs, even physically, he says. This takes her unawares. When she dresses in the morning, she feels, she thinks, like a woman, her heels sufficiently high, her hair sufficiently long, face made up and moderately severe in sunglasses; she doesn't take refuge in gender neutrality. Does she? She thinks that she should be thinking that this is an absurd conversation to be having, a degrading, a humiliating conversation and utterly misplaced, temporally and spatially. And yet she cannot help going on, prodding.

'What is it exactly that I do?' There is an edge to this, perhaps she is fighting back.

'Look at you, playing with your hair. All little girls do that.'

Nervous, she has indeed been winding the spidery ends of a strand of it around one finger. 'And looking down when I speak to you. Can't you hold eye contact? Even a little?' She is torn between anger and primitive sexual response. What has happened to her in five, ten, twelve years? As an undergraduate she would have been outraged, might have machinated to bring about public obloquy for this man's misplaced sexual complacency. Why doesn't she tell him to go to hell? She tells him instead that she often thinks about getting her long hair cut.

But the phrase lodges slyly in the mind. *'Toutes les petites filles font ça.'* Desire, separate from her fury, is now aching and pulsing between her legs, her pants are wet. 'All little girls do that.'

There she is, caught in her childhood bedroom with her hand between her legs, but this voice, now, is paternal, knowing, accepting, reassuring. Or even caught, embarrassed, with her thumb in her mouth, comforting precursor to masturbation. But what is projected in the movie-house of her mind is her current persecutor lying on a bed with a little girl under him, her clothes partially rucked up and back, his trousers open, easing her waistband down, over her sharp little hip bones, caressing, sliding a hand down under her belly, between her legs, and the little girl resisting but finding it difficult to resist this partly delicious sensation, her breath coming hard, surprised and innocent, against his arm, which is crooked under her undeveloped breasts, her heart racing. And he tells her, 'All little girls do this.' Hot with shame at this skilful

148

shifting of blame, she wriggles doubtfully, but only the vestige of her strength remains, and he keeps her firmly in place, groaning into her soft downy neck as little untried cries of pleasure break from her, truly involuntary.

But who is this little girl? Hestia? She does not think so, has never believed that this lies, dormant in her unconscious, waiting to be found. No. This is a little girl known, to Hestia, inside out, in all her small guilts and embarassments, because she has invented her. And yet Hestia can never see her entirely, never truly know her, for the child guards the secret of her face tantalisingly hidden, even from the one who created her, and refuses to be conjured up. Hestia needs to create this child on paper and give her a world, but cannot. She sees wisps of fine blonde hair, sees the expression in the eyes – longing rising like a mist from a marsh – without being able entirely to fix the surrounding features. Too wise to let her in is the child, too sage to let her see. She turns away: Go away, I don't want to talk to you, leave me alone. Maybe she knows, the child, that this woman wants to be her, to step in and take over her soul, and turns her back on Hestia the exploiter, the madam.

Who is Ilona, how did she come into being? For she exists long before Sven takes it into his head to force Hestia's overdue virtue on an early summer evening in south London. Fruit indeed is she of a tear in someone's flesh, but primarily in someone's soul.

Lolita. Ilona. I, i; l, l; o, o; a, a. There is undeniably something of L, o, l, i, t, a in Ilona. But Ilona is not Lo, not Dolly, but Lili, lily-white, lily-pure, sexed only by default, by the involuntary writhings of her fragile body so crudely tricked out of her. Not subject, seductress, willing car pet, but abject. Or is it Ilona-Alice (I, i; l, l; a, a), lost in a strange wonderland? At all events, she is the incarnation of passive beatitude, she embodies an infinity of selfish desire, her quest in life, or her quest in Homesick terms, is and is allowed to be the endless search for self-gratification. She fights her way off Humbert's miasmic lap and back to the breast, and then gives in completely.

Ever unattainable, ever too young, frozen, Ilona is anti-Lolita. Nothing can be asked back of her. She is poised at the point where the one brutal total life-changing soul-heaving shattering has not taken place, and when it does, she will naturally be allowed to bow out.

What Hestia needs to invent, to write, about a little girl, is almost pornographic in its repetitiveness. This is manifest in the phrases which repeat and repeat in consciousness, no matter how often they are written out: probably such a phrase was what began it, for yes, hers is a story of desire, although what she desires has never been, exactly, sex. Hestia's desire for the little girl is quasi-pornographic, too, in that it is never slaked but titillated over and over again. The story running in her head feeds itself and is always hungry; it is written to be read over and over, replayed endlessly in all its small sordid episodes.

What it comes down to is a repeated cry like a needle bumping on an old record, stuck forever in one particular groove. What does Ilona want that Hestia cannot have? The arms of the love object, unconditionally around her. Someone to look after her, love her, feed her, contain her, when everything gets too much and she caves in. Love like a substitute umbilical cord. The caress on the cheek as she falls asleep at night; the almost inaudible click of the lightswitch a second before the door is gently closed.

*

As for marriage, Hestia remembers once, years before in Paris, near the Palais-Royal.

Hestia and Pierre are sitting opposite Daniel and David, who are over for the weekend. This thing with David, Hestia is thinking, and then that 'this thing' gives quite the wrong impression, there is nothing between them, their bonding a convenience to Daniel, only, ensuring harmony between two disparate elements in his existence. But how extraordinarily *nice* David is, she thinks, how smiley, how communicative, searching constantly for eye-contact. And Daniel: there is a moment, over the tea, when he looks at her and Hestia knows that wordless communication still exists between them.

David has just asked Hestia to marry him, in the Louvre, before meeting Pierre for tea. A marriage purely of convenience, allowing David to stay in Britain and qualify as a specialist, without interference from the Home Office, once the statutory marital visit is over. Daniel has been lecturing them expertly on hellenic sculpture,

Hestia and David nudged by this into complicity as his pupils, amused by him, indulgent, admiring his eclectic erudition.

Hestia had stood abstractedly caressing a marble buttock, feeling like a character in a rather racy twenties feminist novel, now published by Virago in a limited edition, and David had put it to her as Daniel, satisfied for now with his account, paused to read more information from the glassed-in panels on the walls. Strolling back over to them, hands in pockets, Daniel had picked up on their conversation.

'We thought of you first,' he says, 'but then we thought you might be a bit – fragile.'

Hestia will take this from Daniel. She asks, 'So who else did you think of?'

'Oh, some dyke in Clapham. She wanted five thousand and use of the house at weekends.'

'I wouldn't accept money,' says Hestia, primly, automatically, but she has long coveted their house.

'That's very decent of you,' says David, formally.

Walking along the Tuileries, close to sunset, under billowing clouds, Hestia's mind runs riot. So much to be lost, or gained; so much to change. What if the Home Office examine her and find that she is a virgin, will the marriage be rendered null and void? She sees pinstriped civil servants in bowler hats and white gloves, crowding courteously around her bed with telescopes and magnifying glasses; she, regal, with her legs spread langourously...

On the one hand, how dare they, her friends, do this, what do they take her for, a piece of flotsam on the tide of life, with no plans, no marital prospects, nothing better to do, and on the other, it is a compliment, they think her pretty enough, plausible; she is to be allowed to play the part of a woman. A decent woman, to all appearances; she and David, living in a big south London house with Daniel, ostensibly the lodger. There will be a wedding with a summer reception in the Balham garden, herself in a severely plain sleeveless dress in old cream lace, high-waisted and narrow, and shoes in some unlikely colour; Pimms and Englishness and laughter and photographs, and the cats watching from the fence, casting their unblinking emerald gaze over the charade that suits them all...

Or will she hear laughter of a different sort, the laugh on she, Hestia? In centuries past she would have been immured in a convent, the unmarriageable daughter, a scourge, a shame, a pity. This is the modern solution to the problem, a *mariage blanc* to a gay Colonial.

But who cares, let the ironic laughter peal out; she will have the house, they cannot refuse her a room in the attic; it will be hers, her kingdom, her home; and in time there will be a child, a little girl, toddling in the immense garden, stealing up to watch the cats watching the frogs leaping in the pond.

Which supposes conjugal rites, of some kind. Hestia is excited by the prospect of both men, in bed, Daniel holding her thighs apart, stroking and calming, while David relieves her of her virginity, forcing a passage in her as yet unyielding flesh, and then relieving her of much more, of her cleanness and her guilt; she wants him to hurt her, abuse her, to satiate. She wants to lie between them, she wants to go to sleep with them among their rough white cotton sheets, with the moon making pale parallelograms on the walls through the thin Japanese blinds...

And the child: Daniel and David will come home from work and play with her, and Hestia will be allowed her time off, to think, to write. In the drawing room, as mistress of the house, lying on the red velvet chaise-longue, drinking tea.

The clouds belly silver light through grey, she has been proposed to, in Paris, at the age of twenty-five, and life is good.

After which there is tea, with Pierre, and the presence of the secret from which he is excluded pulling around the three of them like a slip-knot. Hestia cries all the way through the Woody Allen Pierre takes her to see when the others have gone off for the evening, with sheer and unassuageable longing for Daniel, and with terror at the prospect of the way out, and in, which has just been opened up to her. She cannot touch Pierre that night, cannot bear his homophobic barbs about her friends, pretends to be asleep.

In the end, it is puritan morals that get in the way: to vow before God, or even State, and to know in your heart... . Hestia does not hate herself for this, she despises herself, which is infinitely worse. And in the end, when the law changes, marriage is no longer required, so neither Hestia nor the Dyke from Clapham get charge of the Balham house.

Not to have got in while the chance was there. Hesita-Hestia can barely believe her own stupidity; she could have had it all.

*

Hestia and Daniel have known each other almost ten years when she asks, 'Do you love me as I love you?'

'No.'

In summer, on a rainy day, looking over the Balham garden.

Well, thinks Hestia, you must be made to.

The idea of bequeathing Ilona to him was conceived before even she was.

Everything started from there.

XX

But what, in the final analysis, is the matter with Hestia?

It is impossible, precisely, to answer this question. One can only write round it. There is surrounding space, but nothing at the centre: just as the crux of the female body is a vacant hole, just as there is hollow space in the centre of the human eye.

Younger, she was always afraid of getting the wrong bit, with a tampon, afraid of some shying off, some hideously wrong turning – and could barely even imagine getting anything bigger up there.

Period blood, Hestia tells the gynaecologist, as if the answer had been quite obvious all along, is a path marked out in scarlet, leading from Eve to the Apocalypse, when all the blood of the world will flow...

Pregnant women being ripped open... 'With pain will you give birth to children....' So said the voice, from on high, as she sat by the Sunday effigy of her mother with her dead face and her stiff hat, redundant while the adults took communion, deep in silent prayer, the sun filtering dustily through a high plain window and striking a slant across the inch of blood in her mother's communion glass.

Tiny separate glasses, oddly thimble-shaped, to look as unlike liqueur glasses as possible, Hestia supposed in later life; separate, in racks, for hygiene, rather than passing round a microbe-laden chalice. If I dared, if I only dared, thinks Hestia, at six, at ten, at twelve, take advantage of the moment, dummy-heads bowed, to steal a sip... . That she will go to hell, sooner or later, with or without this, seems a reasonable assumption, for she is not Saved, is not even always convinced that she is Seeking, but she nonetheless believes, blind as a limpet clinging to a rock... In time, she finds out that the blood is blackcurrant juice, not even wine, in case the brethren were to take advantage.

*

Later, in her exile, she exploded into a million pieces; and the bits, perforce, were put back badly, in the wrong order. Once she gave Pierre, for Christmas, a cherry wood puzzle of a heart, and one of the many times she knew she did not love him was when the heart got dislodged from his desk and the pieces dislocated, and he just piled them up, loosely, never bothering to put them back into the tray. She used to dream repeatedly of going back to look for the ghost of herself, younger, on a riverbank, in Durham: some fantasy of wholeness, of integrity.

I want to go back, thinks Hestia, to lie across my single bed late into the suburban summer night reading novels, trailing in empty afternoons between the garden and the piano and the bookcase. Fallow ground, not life, not even making an attempt at it. Instead of having over-hastily to recast the mould, go somewhere else, be somewhere else, transcend, transform, always one step ahead of becoming what you set out to be.

*

'Still the same' can be a euphemism for virginity. She learns this in a Durham coffee shop in a cobbled lane, from a story by Eudora Welty.

*

At school, Hestia had once told Daniel, as the little girls grew inevitably bigger, from one moment to the next, seemingly, Hestia, who had been in the avant-garde, shaving her legs at twelve and buying black garter knickers from Marks and Spencer, telling all her dormitory on a school trip what she had done with her cousin, and genuinely shocking some, knowing what the menarche was and what the average weight-height ratio was to get it, and why you got dysmenorrhea, found herself left behind. By this time they were fourteen, fifteen. Ever since that school had begun, Hestia had been sitting next to Diane, the county javelin champion, the rounded, static goddess and the huntress; a good, compensatory pair. One day in May the history of art group were taken to London, to the National Gallery. Next day it was known, in whispers before Assembly, in the toilets, in the stairwells between classes, that one of their number, Sarah, tall and blonde and brown-eyed without

155

being pretty, and always slightly out of everything, instead of visiting the exhibition, had absconded with a stranger she picked up there, who deprived her of her virginity on Wandsworth Common. She could barely walk, said somebody; that was why she'd skipped PE. It seemed to Hestia that Sarah mostly skipped PE, and that Wandsworth Common was a long way from the National Gallery, and the story quickly became remote, irrelevant. But within the week, Diane, lively, blonde, athletic Diane, had come to Hestia, and asked, with kindness, with a solicitude that was painful after their four-year cohabitation, Diane copying Hestia's French, Hestia always picked for Diane's team in games and allowed to stand around at the back, whether Hestia would mind, if she, Diane, went to sit with Sarah, leaving Hestia with Gwyneth, who was evangelical and wore ankle socks over hairy legs, and whom Hestia needed all her strength to fend off.

Diane and Sarah went to sit with a gradually-expanding group at the back of the class, managing to slump and bask even in navy uniforms among grubbiness and chalk-dust. Years later, coming across a group of female cats on heat, recently-relieved, lying in long grass in a village in the Cévennes, Hestia was reminded of them, of how they were, that year, the summer she was left behind.

Later she learned to disguise it, even to over-compensate. Hetty May, the most highly-sexed virgin in Durham. Hetty sunbathed topless on the college lawn, Hetty came in from lectures with her bra in her pocket, Hetty had handcuffs hanging off her wardrobe door, playing with fire sexually by refusing to acknowledge that fire existed, tempting fate. Bruises for scorch-marks, proof of her womanhood.

Mischanelled, is what she thinks when she looks back on this now. Her libido blocked, and energy spilling out in all the wrong directions. What is it that makes her so patently unable to perform, to do what women do every day, to fuck?

*

There are stories told so many times they become meaningless. Why? they would ask Hestia, doctors, shrinks, friends, and she began to trot out stories which seemed like a sort of truth.

And yet...

Hestia was fifteen when she caught the eye of an English teacher, not her own, but one who taught at the public school to which she would shortly transfer. He went to her parents' church. He had caught her eye many times, she had been fantasising about him for years; at fifteen she looked back in wonderment, almost moved, at the memory of herself at eleven, with bows in her hair, being introduced to him the first time he came to dinner, showing him her guinea-pigs and then being sent to bed.

One Sunday, he asked her back to his school flat 'for a drink', after church, and told her of his struggles against temptation regarding the young girls in his charge, took off her Miss Selfridge dress and got to work on her. Hetty awoke, the day after, feeling as if her life was over. She could see nothing beyond her immediate sorrow; there was pain so bad she didn't go to school, didn't eat, didn't phone her friends. When she did, finally, tell her best friend, Emma, about it, Emma looked up his name in the phone directory to check that he really existed, then sent Hestia a note, in Latin, telling her that all griefs were diminished by time, and then somehow their friendship faded. Not long afterwards, a notice, cut out of *The Telegraph*, appeared on the church notice board, announcing his forthcoming marriage to someone with a double-barrelled name. Hestia came home from church and tried to tell this to her mother, who said 'Do we have to discuss that man every time we're on our own?'

It was more than a decade later that she remembered: his disapproval of her cotton underwear, him coming before he'd even got his trousers off and having to go and change before driving her home to her parents and telling her savagely to get out of his car before they saw him.

*

Hestia, at eighteen, au-pairing one summer in the south of France, went out with a boy as dark as a gypsy, a beautiful, anarchic boy, who drove where he wanted to go, regardless of the lack of roads, sometimes with his right hand between her thighs. Whenever he came to her bed, Hestia would spread a towel across the mattress.

157

Why she did so was unclear even to herself, as there was nobody to interfere, or even notice; she had her own entrance in a yellow-stone courtyard, with lemon trees. By the end of her stay, she had disposed of six of her mother's bathtowels in this way, because she did not know where to wash them without bringing on herself unspeakable shame, the family washing-machine being in the kitchen, and controlled by the mistress of the house. She had been forced to invent an extra holdall, bought in Montpellier, lost in transit, and her mother had insisted that she claim on her insurance, for what was allegedly mislaid.

*

There was a story Hestia's mother would tell, ostensibly about how she didn't like to be alone in the house. There had been a family wedding when she was a girl of seventeen, and they were a large family, in the East End. For reasons which were never clear, she had found herself alone in the family home on the night after the wedding, and her aunt, whose daughter was the bride, rang up and told her to come over and eat up the remains of the feast, not to stay in that big house by herself. She could have the room where the couple had stayed the previous night before leaving for the honeymoon; she, Aunt Liza, hadn't got round to changing the sheets what with one thing and another, but she wouldn't mind that. This was an order, not an invitation, apparently: and yet what was curious was that this was not the point of the story, which puzzled Hestia more and more as, growing older, she heard it repeated. It could have been an anecdote about being made to sleep in somebody else's bridal sheets, it could have been a story against the slatternly ways of Aunt Liza. But the way it was told it was neither of these things; it was simply about being alone in the house and not liking it, and the kindheartedness of this aunt in the East End. Any association of the bridal sheets with the loss of virginity, or with sex of any sort, traces of semen and blood, had been edited out of the story, out of the experience, even, apparently, in retrospect.

*

And thinking of her father, Hestia sees a blind in her head coming down with a rattle and a click. Who is pulling the blind? What mustn't be seen?

What was it her father could not bear to look at?

*

Hestia, as a grown-up woman, is not quite sure that she has the right to put on make-up, to wear beautiful clothes; she doesn't feel at ease with her body, feels grotesque, as if play-acting only, and about to be sharply told off for getting all those clothes out, and making a mess of her face. There is, still, the tyrannical voice that says, petulant, You're not wearing make-up, you're not going out, don't think you're a woman, young lady, because you're not...

Hestia, at nineteen, leaving a casual lover's room, in the castle at Durham at five a.m., finds that she has lost her keys, and can't get back into her room where her white bed waits under the paradoxical crimson ceiling, and is condemned to wander around, hands in her pockets, no loose change, until the porter comes on duty at seven, and it is in that dawn, in the silent empty Bailey, that she discovers the ultimate loneliness of sex.

XXI

Hestia once more takes up her blackbound notebook:

*Maybe I can't let a man through the barrier for his own protection.
Maybe some hideous monster coils within... Something that has to be
vomited out, daily, placating the gods of wrath and destruction...
Maybe if I let him in, the monster will bite it off, his thing.*

*The spasms, the fluttering-up, the helpless involuntary flinching –
The shame –
Down, wantons, down.
What if they were to come OUT?*

If I had a penis, sometimes I suspect it would be erect all the time.

*If you can get through without touching and being touched, you may
just be ok, you might escape the punishment to come. And so the body
takes over, not the mind, clenches its own gates, creates its own
barrage.*

*Dream: that if I let myself be penetrated, my mother would bore a
hole in my stomach.*

*Penetration. It would be like taking a breadknife and piercing the
papers stretched taut and unbroken across the top of a new jar of
coffee.*

Shutters. Curtains. Beef curtains...

Not to be able to open that mouth, to speak with it, to breathe...

*I remember myself – right at the end of being a student, in Durham,
in the dilapidated vicarage, with the view across the river to the rose
window. There was a night, after Finals, when unable to take in
freedom, life, the future, drunk on Proust and Colette and Gide and*

Dorothy Richardson, I lay naked in the early hours on my single bed and felt that I had all my life, all my time. I remember feeling: Look up, and read your position off whatever chart holds it... Now I feel as if I am off the chart. I don't know how to live like other people.

The girls at school, when there was a craze for psychological tests, said, 'You're in a dark room, no doors, no windows, no way out. There's just a bed. What do you do?' I said, 'I lie down and go to sleep'...

The sound of the light being switched off, before you go to sleep.

The door shutting, into silence, into a silent room.

Next day, what she tells her analyst is this:

The little girl, herself, aged ten, is on holiday, staying with her grandparents in Broadstairs, a paradise of mussel-stalls and tacky souvenir shops and sea bathing; fish and chips on the beach, milkshakes sucked through curly straws like three-dimensional treble clefs, and visits to her sister, glamorous at seventeen as a waitress in the big hotel on the front, where she has an attic room. It is on one of these visits to Ruth in her time between shifts, clattering up the uncarpeted spiral staircase and bursting in without knocking, full of the excitement of having found a dead, but perfect, octopus on one of her solitary trips to the beach, that Hetty is undone: she throws the door open and confronts something too big in her sister's bed, which for a long moment she fails to make sense of, a bulk moving clumsily and not quite rhythmically under the light summer covers. The room smells of sweat and of something Hetty does not recognise, and she flees, running back down to the beach, gasping for fresh air.

That afternoon, walking along the promenade with the creeping unpleasant feeling of being in disgrace, Hetty is nearly swept out to sea by a freak wave, a wall of glassy grey moving so inexorably towards her that it scarcely seems to be moving at all. Its arrival holds her in such fascination that she cannot stop looking, with no idea of what is coming towards her, out of the blue.

Luckily, as the first aid lady on the beach and her grandparents and later the doctor all tell her, instinct and fear make her clutch the railings of the promenade in front of her, duck her head and hang on, mouth somehow closed against the heaving weight of water.

Her sister comes to see her that evening, tucks her into bed, lets her borrow her make-up and listen to her new records.

Nothing is said about the other episode, but somehow they remain linked in Hestia's mind.

'Frameless stories, like rimless spectacles,' says Hestia to Dr X, and he smiles.

'Go on with them,' he says, and then, 'Why is it you're so terrified of sex? Why does it seem like this great, slapping wave that knocks you over?'

'I don't know,' says Hestia. 'I can only answer that question with another image. Also on holiday, also by the sea.'

'Go on.' Hestia's narrative needs these small encouragements, she is never wholly sure of its legitimacy, its worth.

A little girl, still small and formless, on a seaside holiday in Wales, picking sea anemones from rocks lustrous with slime at the fag-end of a cloudy dusk, after a wettish day. The anemones, unlike the stubborn and finally tedious limpets, will yield satisfactorily to a gentle prod into their spherical rubbery shine, although carefully sadistic gradations from barely perceptible to vicious yield disappointingly little variation in response. They are globular and incarnadine, like some silent and sinister message from the future lying packed and hidden in the little girl's womb. Her stealthy investigations, though blameless of this knowledge, are not innocent.

The evening is fading, has reached precisely that stage where, deep in a book indoors, you would at last be forced in irritation to get up and switch on the light. Small boats bob lethargically in the brownish and slightly malodorous harbour. There is a gnawing void in the little girl's solar plexus, all her being has become a dragging weight. She looks up to see her sisters and her mother gathered round a further pool, possibly sufficiently interesting to bring the little girl back to life. She needs to feel the snap of the hypnotist's fingers an inch from her face. With cries of mock-disgust and pleasure and little quacks of bursting air, they are popping the blisters in a long frond of seaweed. Bladderwrack. And before she know what has happened to her, the little girl is aware of the warm rush of pee on the insides of her legs, and then she is stretched on the sand, half-winded by the enormous blow which has just ricocheted from her mother's hand. Everything is damp and cold, her face, the sand, her skirt, her sandshoes; her insides are outside, and the little girl is drenched with shame. When she gets up she says, 'When are we going home? I want to go home.'

'OH!' exclaims the mother. It is practically a roar. 'What's the *matter* with you? Why are you such a misery-guts?'

And the sisters, united in disparagement and self-approval, glare.

*

'Do you think I should have a hymenectomy?' asks Hestia of the doctor when she has finished, by way of not answering the question which triggered this narrative. 'Ask the gynaecologist to cut it out?'

Dr X looks at her gravely. 'I couldn't advise it,' he says.

'Like Jeeves,' says Hestia, and takes herself off with her cultural reference floating in the void.

XXII

But walking home through the chill evening in dull, respectable Strasbourg, between the tall, sheltered, shuttered lamp-lit houses and the prostitutes loitering in the moonlight, Hestia decides to act.

She feels stuck in childhood, remote; she half-suspects that this is why she is unable to make contact, with men casually introduced to her or carefully chosen, in cafés and bars and *winstubs*. For form's sake, she goes out with friends and suffers the attentions of the single men who float around, opportunistic as they eye her curves, circumspect when she opens her mouth, fading away altogether as, giving up, she keeps it closed. What is worse, things are beginning to scare and jar on her, things that have nothing to do with sex at all. Crowded buses. Lifts. Locked doors. Something has to be done. If she can just solve the one, the central, problem, maybe things will fall into place.

Within forty-eight hours, another appointment is made and kept.

The gynaecologist has given her an article to read. Having absorbed it, she is supposed to prepare herself for her hymenectomy, the clinical removal of her hymen under local anaesthetic, and go back to see him.

I have never, ever felt less like having sex than after reading this, thinks Hestia. The author adopts a highly antipathetic tone, towards women, towards her, she feels targeted, blamed. The woman is referred to throughout as 'the patient'.

Vaginismus is the most frequent cause of unconsummated marriages. Very often, the spasm of the patient's perivaginal muscles is not the only obstacle to intromission. Either from the outset, or after a failed and painful attempt at penetration, the obstacle of the closure of the thighs by defence reflex for phobic fear of infraction is manifest. This barrage, in fact created by the anal muscles, may cause the husband to fail for many months....

What husband, thinks Hestia, and in what possible sense could it said to be his hypothetical 'failure', his pain?

And, reading further, *clitorise*. What sort of a verb is that? The author points out that in what he insists on calling 'standard vaginismus' the woman has been known to 'clitorise without reticence', and to indulge in 'efficacious masturbation'. What the hell, wonders Hestia, is 'efficacious' masturbation? And 'standard vaginismus' – the phrase profoundly irritates her; what is supposed to be standard about it? What is ordinary or banal about a blocked passage, an aperture that won't open? Nothing going in or out, is that supposed to be a 'standard' way to live?

The article decrees that she will have to have an examination, designated an 'inspection', to rule out any 'gross anatomical anomaly'. What is the punishment, if you don't pass? But she is being punished already...

The problem does not indicate a monstrosity, states the article. Oh yes it does, thinks Hestia, darkly. Nobody has ever proved that where it counts, she is a woman; nobody has ever been there. Up there, in there, she could be anything.

According to this information, the gynaecologist will 'put' her in a foetal position – on her back, but curled up, knees drawn up to her chin, once more like Klimt's Danae, although she cannot run to those hanks of red hair curtaining the marbled shoulders – place a 'friendly' hand on her thigh – and inspect her. Somewhere, thinks Hestia, all the look-but-don't-touch stuff, legitimised, probably pleases her, appeals to her regressive and exhibitionistic tendencies. No wonder Danae is secretly smiling.

She is further informed that she lacks the 'determination' that it takes, and that most women possess, to get through – ha, thinks Hestia – the first penetration...

She puzzles for a long time over 'assiduous scissoring'.

Scissoring? She wouldn't call it – when she finally realises what it must be – assiduous. Somewhere there are dim memories, rather, of trying to rub one's thighs together secretly, provoking sensation without appearing to move – doing it while pretending it wasn't happening, on buses, at school, in bed. 'Thighs locked together,' says the article, contradicting the scissor image, locked shut: and Hestia sees in her head a woman in a prison-cell, banging her head against the bars in frustration. The first time she masturbated, at fourteen, on a June night, she remembers the surprise of orgasm, the sheer forbidden overwhelmingness of it, the whirling stars in her head; afterwards she fainted – with guilt. And yet her legs had been together, and in her head, she saw Victorian girls, and boys, forced into chastity belts, some image picked up from a half-watched documentary, their entrances and exits locked away, a danger from which their owners had to be protected.

Now, the article pronounces that the examination should go ahead, in spite of her possible protests – she is horrified at this: rape. But not only that: will you stop if I say so, will you stop if it gets too bad? – This has always been her talisman – her way of coping with threats, physical, sexual – and it also applies to life itself: she has long had an arrangement with herself that if it all gets too much, too bad, she will disappear in a metaphorical hot-air balloon, gently severing the umbilical cord that attaches her to life; suicide, that dangerous and beautiful word. And then when it comes to it, every time, she realises how very difficult it is, even in its practicalities; tablets are not guaranteed to work; the best way is to slit your wrists, length-ways, drink a great deal of alcohol, lie in a hot bath with the light off and wait to die. But she does not, when it comes to it, want to bleed her way out of existence, like a Bayonne pig...

The article tells her she has to push, and she has no idea of how to translate this imperative into her body. Women push in labour, but she has never been able to imagine exactly how, where, with what; all of which comes circularly back to, perhaps she is just not a woman... and not having this awareness, this control, makes her feel oddly disgusting, as if she is not mistress of her own bodily functions: even if the problem concerns things going in, rather than things coming out. Ingress and egress seem to unite against her, to become one, circling round to join one another, as in the thesaurus, as if to avoid being *unopened, unopeanable, shut, shuttered, bolted, barred, locked, stoppered, corked, obturated, unpierced, imperforate, unholed, nonporous, impervious, impermeable, were to be unclosed, unstopped, uncapped, uncorked, unshut, ajar, unbolted, unlocked, admitting, accessible, wide-open, agape, gaping...*

There is an illogical equation in her head: if she lets herself go, if she lets anything come in, everything will spill out, warm, stinking liquids, entrails, intestines. She always feels, these days, as if she is about to fall apart at the seams, straps falling from shoulders, hair perpetually streaming from its chignon.

Even at the end of the article, when in the author's scenario glowing couples return to give thanks to the gynaecologist, she notices, the woman is still 'the patient'. But she knows that she has to go against any notion of feminist principles if she wants to be helped; it seems to be one or the other.

Hestia goes to her appointment with the gynaecologist with a quite astonishing array of chemicals, both inside her and in her handbag. Valium, herbal tranquillisers, two types of pre-emptive painkillers, already ingurgitated, a tube of anaesthetic gel, which, in the toilet, she vaguely aims somewhere between her legs; the box from the chemist's with the sealed syringe in it for the anaesthetic injection, tablets to slow the bleeding. In his room there are no stirrups; you sit in a chair which holds your legs apart and are smoothly tilted backwards and pumped up to the right angle. Once installed, Hestia breathes deeply, this she has learned to do, with her diaphragm; thus far, she has been a good pupil. She can fill her head with darkness at will, make her being a mere dot on the surface of a dense, immense black globe, some trick with the mind and the eye, the mind's eye. In so far as she is thinking of anything at all, her conscious mind is registering pleasure at the senstaion of her spread legs, at the firm muscles of her inner thighs, at her clean thick hair falling in her own face and almost in the gynaecologist's when he comes in and levers the chair upright, so that he can talk her through it. She is wishing to feel desire in her vagina, but the wish is not being transmitted to her flesh. Forward, she is excited, maybe even behind, but there: nothing. No feeling at all.

He puts on a finger condom, tilts her back again, slips a forefinger inside her, stops. Hestia breathes harder; her heart is starting to race. She wants him to stroke her hair, but cannot say so. He prods a little more, meets resistance, Hestia's sealed and superfluous flesh.

She grits her teeth; she wants this, is desperate for it to succeed, but where there had been no vestige of feeling, there is now a distinct pain; she can put up with it if he does not move.

They stay like that, Hestia concentrating on her yogic breathing.

He tells her to relax, praises her when she manages it, pats her left foot and calls her a good girl. She thinks that perhaps it is beginning to begin to be possible, but the weight of what is happening to her is appalling.

The phone rings, he takes his finger out. His daughter's school, she gathers, and knows she wants to be this daughter. At the same time, she wants, as she lies with her legs fixed apart, to cry out in abandon, Suck my cunt... . When he puts the phone down, he comes back and takes up where he left off, parting her lips, working fast now, inserting the injection: this hurts, excruciatingly; Hestia screams as it goes in, gasps as it remains. And then she makes the mistake of opening her eyes and looking at what is to come – at the long steel scissors. He is pressing down on her, forcing her apart now, forcing her to stay in place. Five, ten seconds and it's over, he tells her, and in the moment he speaks, her legs fly out of the chair with a compulsive spasm, and she has kicked him, hard, in the chest, knocking the scissors out of his hand. They spin across the floor.

She is shaking uncontrollably. 'I didn't do that. It wasn't me; it wasn't me.' He puts a hand on her shoulder and pats it as she sits, half-naked – he is a good doctor and a good man – and tells her that she isn't ready yet, that it doesn't matter.

It does, oh how it does, cries Hestia inwardly, virgin goddess imprisoned in her flesh. Never, it will never happen; if it can't be done surgically, it will never, ever happen.

'Can I have a general anaesthetic? Please?'

'I can't do that, and any surgeon who does is a charlatan. You have to be ready for it; you have to participate. If not, it's not the breaking of the hymen that will solve the problem.'

Out of nowhere, she suddenly thinks of something she had once read about prisoners being executed by lethal injection: they were advised to be co-operative, to participate in bringing about their own death.

She had wanted to be fascinated by the flow of her own hymenal blood. She had wanted him to clamp a towel between her legs, and then her own hand over the towel, passing responsibility for her own body back to her, and to say, 'Aren't you going to get dressed?' as she stood in wonder. And now, nothing but obloquy, the failure to perform, the failure even to be able to be wounded and to bleed... .

In anger, and frustration and disappointment, she stops on the way home and buys a cucumber, and, once home, peels it, sculpts it, squeezes and bruises it into wet slipperiness, tries to get it inside herself, and fails; the gates are well and truly barred and there is nothing her conscious mind can do to unlock them.

There is still a point of extreme soreness from the injection. She masturbates herself into a frenzy, hurting and rubbing the sore place on purpose; in her head she sees herself whipped, pilloried, humiliated. Savagely, she crunches her teeth into the cucumber dildo. Her stomach heaves.

'Push!' he had told her, 'as if you were going to pass a stool.' What an appalling expression, Hestia had thought; far worse than anything overtly scatalogical. And besides, somewhere this is what she is afraid of. Falling apart at the seams, not coping, not controlling, everything falling out, ending in a bath of blood and viscera and entrails. To be fucked is, somewhere, to be disembowelled. Come forward for disembowelling, she had heard, when she got off the ferry once at Folkstone, instead of disembarkation, and that was the moment at which, in horror, she had known what was inside her.

Weeks after the failed hymenectomy, on the metro in Paris, the phrase — Push, as if you were going to pass a stool — comes back into her head. She still doesn't know what to do. Intellectually she sees, but it doesn't register in this woman's body that she doesn't know how to inhabit. Open, shut, open, shut; it should be automatic, like the mechanism of an umbrella. Open and shut; get laid, then lay.

In a department store on the Rue de Rivoli, she finds a basket of polystyrene eggs, the size of hen's eggs, looks at them idly, wondering what possible use they could be put to, buys a handful anyway, and then, having bought them, knows. In a changing cubicle, she slips one inside her knickers, the pointed end just inside her. Now there is pleasure, she thinks, of a sort. She wiggles the fat end of the egg with a finger and is amazed at the sensation; in spite of her efficacious masturbation, this is like the intimation of a new dimension. She pushes, half-heartedly, but it doesn't go up more than half an inch. Nonetheless, Hestia walks out with the egg still held in place by her knickers, but isn't really surprised when, halfway down the escalator at Hôtel de Ville, it bounces out from under her skirt. She bursts out laughing, the acid laughter of bitter irony, not amusement, and the people who notice the falling egg take it for some kind of joke, or dare.

Hestia: a virgin without a reason, a goddess without a myth, wrapped in a fairy-tale enchantment: maybe she never wanted to be pricked, at bottom, never wanted to wake up.

*

As for love, Hestia loves her shrink, Dr X, comforter, wiper away of a hundred thousand tears, holding, making whole, looking into her face with ineffable tenderness, eliciting great sighs of relief; healer, revealer, the sun, the moon, the stars and comets.

For him, for him only, she could part her legs; he already knows her inside out. And backwards.

XXIII

Hestia, in the night; what to fantasise? Her store of images is empty, between her legs she is bone dry; she can no longer fantasise herself into childhood, pre-pubescence, and she does not know how to fantasise her womanhood, what to dream, what to wish for. Going back to the old habits no longer does anything for her, there is boredom, rather than disgust, like picking up a book in a prison cell read and reread for the thousandth time...

There used to be a time when she longed for her own silky childish skin, the lightness of her limbs lying in bed, the flatness of her chest and buttocks. No more, and yet she feels imprisoned in the body she has, encumbered by it, unsure how to treat it, how to move it, what to do with it. She no longer knows what it is for.

Ilona

XXIV

The trip to Baden-Baden is Ilona's reward for allowing Daniel to go away, as well as the promised change of scene after her convalescence and the removal of her plaster, a journey together before he undertakes his own, thus making journeys seem less terrible. Daniel arranges it as a luxury, as a supreme treat, a first class sleeper in the train up through France to Strasbourg, where they will hire a car. He has bought her a fine grey angora wrap for the occasion, bringing it home from Printemps in a shiny flat white gift box, and she cuddles into it, luxuriously. They have brought, organising it between them, maps and guidebooks to the Black Forest: the journey is also to be educational, for Ilona has a thirst for being educated, at least by Daniel.

Always pleased to sleep in the same space as her protector, Ilona lies smiling in the top bunk and gives herself up to the light and shadow chasing across the ceiling, to the incessant muted rattle of the train's movement, to the occasional screeching into stations with bleaching light and people coming and going on platforms, mingling with her dreams, but who needn't be bothered about, because shut safely out...

Daniel takes Ilona to Freiburg, to the Titisee, to Constance, to ride on pleasure-boats and to walk, and they save the utter lethargy of immersion in the springs for the evenings, sinking to the neck into hot mineral-smelling water as if into the womb, outside, under trees, in the almost-dark, with the steam rising in billows and wraiths among the leaves, an intermittent, irregular moon, and nothing else visible at all. At the hotel, Daniel has booked a room with a double bed for himself and a smaller bed for her on a raised mezzanine, under the eaves, hemmed in by scrolled railings, a home from home, he says. Exhausted by the waters, they both sleep the sleep of the dead, and look out in the morning on a pink church-spire, the colour of fondant icing, and a pastel town, unreal, rising along the curves of the Black Forest beyond. They take the train back to Strasbourg to see the cathedral, managing even in the forty-minute trip to fit in apple strudel and coffee, with damask cloths and silver cutlery, in the restaurant car, with a great fuss made of Ilona by the young Czech waiter, and they go to see the house where Hestia had lived in a two-roomed apartment, and where Daniel had stayed, several times. But Ilona goes stiff and silent at this, and they leave, quickly.

The trip is on the whole a success; Ilona is transparently delighted with everything he proposes, and there is no tension now between them. They are in harmony, happy together. Neither is there any repetition of what happened in Nice, after the accident, or even any reference to it.

*

Nevertheless, shortly after their return to the south, Daniel goes away. He silently bundles his cases out onto the terracotta-tiled landing and down to the waiting taxi before the dawn, for it has been agreed that this will make it easier for Ilona. With no parting tussle, she will simply wake up to Richard, who will have given her something the previous evening to calm her down and make her sleep, and, it is hoped, prevent her from waking up to despair, and who will, that Sunday, take her out and spoil her.

The first thing that presents itself to Ilona's inner vision when she wakes is a picture, quite clear and unmuddied, of a large wood-framed egg-timer, which has just flipped up the other way, the hard way; the first grains of sand barely beginning to trickle through, so fine you hardly see them fall.

The panic has subsided. What she feels now is a grim resolution. Time without Daniel stretches like a prison-sentence.

Ilona sits and waits, a princess looking out of the window of her tower. Something which could be read as disdain, but which is not quite that, creeps into her manner. It is more a question of not wanting to touch or be touched by the world, the better to concentrate on waiting. There are more than fifty days to go.

Perhaps these will be more manageable when she has succeeded in knocking off two or three of them, by keeping herself quite still and undistracted, and making sure that the sand is trickling truly and regularly in its infinitely narrow pass...

Daniel phones, touching down at the airport in Singapore, then from his hotel in Tokyo, and then daily, which becomes increasingly difficult as his movements become less predictable and more complicated. At weekends, when Ilona is shuttled off to Paris to stay with Richard by Brigitte or Sabine, on the few occasions when Daniel doesn't phone, and sometimes when he does, Ilona sits in Richard's arms, letting him rock her, desperate for this contact and yet a little cold, a little distant, pretending somewhere inside herself that she is not after all sitting on the knee of this non-Daniel, that she feels no desire at all to reach up and put her arms around this foreign neck, or to bury her face in this sandy wiry hair...

She longs for Daniel's hair, separate, silky, blonder, falling over his face, and is somewhere ashamed to find comfort in this other beating heart.

XXV

Durham; the room on the Bailey with the tiger shutters.

19th February 1990. Daniel got back at two o'clock this morning, having bought a Saab in London and driven up... He's looking very pale and tired today; however, we've finally had our chat. I've just finished riding, briefly (?), a big wave of depression. I spotted him at lunch – I ate in college – and went down to his room afterwards to ask whether we, or whether he, were still going to see As You Like It *in Newcastle tomorrow: the reply was yes, and that we'll drive over, and that he does want to go; this he rather spoilt by asking who else was going. No point tormenting myself over this. Anyway – this is all very jumbled – he said he'd come up for coffee after supper, and appeared, indeed while Cara was her, and behaved in a flirtatious sort of way, as he does. Cara soon left... and there we were.*

It was comfortable – me sitting with my feet up on my desk, he in the armchair, sitting across it, effortlessly graceful. Outside it was raining, I had the sash window open wide. That it was so peaceful was his excuse for not telling me, once again, what he'd been going to. But in the end I said – what if I already know? – to which he said, naturally enough, Know what, so I said, That you prefer men? And we talked. I told him about the two and a half possibilities I'd formed after Candlemass: a girlfriend in Durham – a girlfriend back home – or that. He said, I could be impotent. We laughed. Or tried to.

It was an intimate and an honest discussion; afterwards, though, or indeed during, I felt I was being tactless. I did try to understand... He didn't seem to mind talking about it – I think the difficulty as far as he perceived it lay in telling me... And remembering how I reacted when I first found out – real shock – he was probably right.

Maybe I should congratulate myself on a successful rescue operation.

But a singularly painful one.

He doesn't prefer men, thinks Ilona. He prefers me. She leafs back in her mother's hard-bound diary; she wants to read about Candlemass, whatever that was.

So here we are again, the night of the ball, Candlemass, me bleeding copiously. Still in my jeans, and they're all coming round at six; I haven't done anything yet.

They, Ilona notes – Hestia is going to a ball with 'they', not 'him'.

There's going to be a total eclipse of the moon within the next half hour and at the moment, it's hanging there, as Coleridge would say, quietly, across the spread of the gardens and the river and Kingsgate and Elvet Riverside, streaked, smoke on white in a bright blue evening sky, outrageously beautiful, unutterably serene.

Then on a new page and in a much wilder hand:

What, simply, confuses me is that this time, as opposed to a lifetime of other times, every time I looked in the mirror the image that came back to me was perfect. The dress, beautiful, my waist slim and muscled, my pectorals firm, hair just cut, heels high, make-up ok to good, and a general air of confidence.

The script now tiny and controlled.

You have to do a pretty quick rescue operation because you cannot be that sad. You cannot let the pain gnaw. You have to take positive action: don't say anything or imply anything about it to anyone else, assume complete blandness, and talk to him. You know him well enough for that. Blame it all on yourself and talk to him.
I cannot feel like this. When I got home I went to bed, and felt this to be a remarkable achievement, because what I wanted to do was roll around the floor, howling with pain. I cannot let the pain come because there is no possibility of dealing with it.
Afterwards, Cara, in my dark red room, stroking my hair; I discovered that one never runs out of tears – oh, crying, what a cathartic experience, if you give yourself up to it, wholly, if you enter into your pain and let it live and only it.

This will go down as the height of passion, ha [savagely underlined], *of all feeling, the superb double pinnacle of pleasure and pain, sublime. The mirror, my nakedness, ripping the dress off over my head, then my underwear, standing between him and the door, naked, a challenge. It will never mend. He pushed me aside and said, I think we should talk about this in the morning, then closed the door and left. And in the morning he had disappeared, no answer from his room, letters not taken from the lodge.*

How do you deal with pain, what do you do with it? Just cling with surprise, with gratification, to the image of yourself in that now-ravaged dress.

Feeling, walking through town, or even sitting in lectures, as if I'm watching another version of myself, far off, howling, curled up and howling with pain, and also with rage.

(Next day). Feeling better I think today. Yesterday was a day of convalescence. I stayed, mostly, in bed till 4pm, thinking about getting up to have a bath but unable to do so; listening to the radio, and doing only that, realising at one point that the whole of Mozart's 38th symphony and all the Pictures at an Exhibition had gone by since I'd last had une intention quelconque *– get up, have a bath, eat, drink. I was trying very hard to unwrap my head from the shroud of infected memory which had tangled round it in the night; I was trying to set my mind in neutral, to show that I could. But feeling most horribly betrayed.*

Cara was kind and soft and dark and comforting. Going to sleep I felt some relief. And when morning came, felt better – . Nonetheless, a day of wound-licking. There was a residual stickiness around the eyes, and, for most of the day, a feeling of slight unsteadiness – .

(Later). Finally, after the shaking, the staring rigid into darkness, the tears wrenched out, there comes a point where it all seems too ridiculous, altogether unlikely.

Make the week spring away from disaster. But I am torn between the desire for reconciliation and the need to make my point, to see him and be cold and hurt but proud. You know, Hetty, you know perfectly damn well, that if you avoid him, ignore him, this is only to make sweeter the day, the minute, the moment, when you slip up to him at

*the bar or in the Bailey, and smile at him the way you know you smile
at him...*

*This morning I was sitting on the edge of my bed, drying my hair,
naked. My thighs were spread, and I was sitting on the base of my
spine, as cats do, when you stretch them out vertically on your lap for
stroking, so that my legs were closed and tense, so that my stomach-
muscles were taut, and bending my head to dry my hair upside down
I was struck by the beauty, the firmness, the shapeliness, of this view
of my own body. Then found myself in grinding, tearing tears – . But
still believe I looked beautiful in my dress.*

*I remember – with pain – in Frontignan, a year ago, standing
being kissed – mouth, breasts, shoulders – by Franck, in the sea, in
the dawn.*

*Dreams: so obvious as to be almost ridiculous. In one I was just
about to kiss Daniel when he cried, 'It's suppressed.' Oh, the
projection of my desires... In another, his flesh was feminine,
somehow, when actually he's firm, broad, muscular.*

*In all this I've said nothing about the play, which was both
riotous and beautiful; all that gender-bending in the clockless
forest...*

This last goes over Ilona's head, but she perseveres.

*...I feel – appallingly, abjectly – rejected, still. Perversely, feeling
privileged, maybe, that he was talking to me about the man he's
going to see in London.*

*Take what there is if there's nothing else on offer. Something very
tender in his voice, telling me about this man. He was obviously quite
excited about the whole idea, wanting to be asked. He says that when
he goes to see some of his friends in London, all gay, it gives him a
feeling in his stomach... I loved him for that. Apparently, Daniel was
sexually innocent until the age of nineteen – hadn't been out with
girls before he knew he was gay. And the boys he fell for at school
had never measured up to his expectations....*

Then, later, in a different volume, this:-

The river bank in Durham, with Daniel, the woods spreading out steeply down to the river below college. We were on our way up to Edinburgh to see the Durham Players do some gay classic at the fringe and were going to spend the night in John Street, in the house he'd be moving into in the autumn, under the viaduct. I was coming up from Birmingham, he from London, and we were supposed to meet in the train at York, but we'd missed each other somehow.

Arriving in Durham alone in the dark, I was afraid: Durham in late summer, empty of students, felt oddly foreign and potentially hostile. I felt dangerously conspicuous. Did we finally meet up by accident? I don't remember. But we still had our rucksacks when the story starts. Daniel wanted to go into college to get some cuttings for his garden; we had already been scrabbling in the earth on Prebends, to gather plants. None of this we considered in any way akin to stealing – we were part of Durham, it grew on us, we grew on it, there was a feeling of the earth being at least symbolically ours, for the time we were there; but for entry into college, at night, in the vacation, by this time in our undergraduate careers at least minimal subterfuge was required. The student-administrated anarchy of the first year or so had been quashed; there was a new porter, possibly unfriendly.

Daniel left me on the river bank, below college, with the rucksacks, while he scrambled up the bank – there was no real path and no lighting – through the trees and so into the bottom of the college gardens. As the footsteps faded I became aware of the silence and the intensity of the darkness spread through the trees above. But waited, calmly enough, at least at first. Then finally there came the sound of footsteps zig-zagging their way down the bank, and relief flooded. I began calling Daniel's name, I must have called several times.

Daniel... I'm here. No answer. I could hear my own voice becoming puzzled and desperate. The footsteps kept on coming, nearer and nearer, nearer still. Then suddenly, from much higher up, an answering voice, Daniel beginning the descent, still quite a long way up through the dark. In my stomach I felt something clench froggily...

Did Daniel hurry and get to me first?

Did the alien footsteps veer away?

I don't remember. I remember afterwards, in John Street, Daniel

bedding out the cuttings in the tiny fenced-off square of garden
under the railway line in the light from the kitchen, me going very
quiet and feeling a sudden urge first to clean the bathroom, which
was not very clean from the previous students, although we were only
there for one night. There was no hot water. I heated pans and kettles
and had some sort of a bath. I'd left some hot water on the cooker top
for a bath for Daniel too, but he let it go cold. Later I lay in the
single bed in the room next to Daniel's and listened to my heart race
with fear...

This story bothers Ilona without her being able to put her finger on why. As well it may. Is it the disappearance into the dark of one person, one beloved person, and the re-emergence of another, a threatening stranger, wordless? Or is it the sinister, possibly vicarious, washing ritual afterwards? Who or what was it that Hestia was trying to wash away? And under all this is something else, more threatening, some suggestion, not explicit: two people crossing paths in an impenetrably dark forest on a late-summer night. What had they gone there for? What were they doing? Some intersection, lost to this narrative of the story, some encounter. That it may not have been that particular night, with the owner of those particular footsteps, is not the point. Is Ilona, with the tattered volume still open in front of her, unaware, or not entirely and not coherently aware, of these things? Who can tell?

XXVI

When time, after all, passes, Ilona is amazed to find months have turned to weeks and weeks to days and days, at last, to hours. Richard is there as he has been for all the intervening weekends, except when Ilona has been to him in Paris, and with Brigitte and Catherine they are organising Daniel's Welcome Home party. Ilona has occupied not a few grains of the sandy trickle of her time, recently, in inventing Daniel's present, his cake. She has for weeks been making him a wide, shallow fruit bowl, decorated with generous loopy glazed ochre flowers, in Pottery – one of the few classes in which she is happy – and she has finally solved the problem of the cake, which has to be an unforgettable, an inimitable cake. Ilona, trained by Hestia, is good at cooking of all sorts, and she has found a heart-shaped mould lying forgotten in one of the cavernous cupboards of the Nice flat. She decides, finally, on plain chocolate frosting, onto which she will paint freehand in white icing a stylised map of Daniel's route, putting a chocolate plane in the centre. She has seen chocolate planes in the window of a master chocolatier in town; the elements have presented themselves, and the plan has come together. The fruit bowl lacks only its last glaze.

Ilona believes she has changed, altered immeasurably, since Daniel has been away. Time, initially so intractable, has after all unfolded, has moved; she has stopped counting the days. She believes without quite having articulated this that she has learned to live without him, and this is why, when he reappears out of the blue, on foot at the school gates, too dazed to drive after his long journey, hours early after all, having managed a connection in Paris more favourable than anticipated, unshaven, a little rough around the edges and the more beautiful for it, Ilona rushes at him, throws herself into his waiting arms, bursts into tears and sobs that she has missed him, and then feeling his arms tight around her, suddenly pulls away and goes shy and all but refuses to speak to him. He turns into a café to take her for a drink, so she can have him to herself before they get back to the celebrations, and he her, and she answers him in

183

monosyllables, sipping her grenadine, eyes on the table. Failing to will his gaze under her eyelashes and compel her to look up, Daniel leans forward and pushes her hair back from her still-damp cheeks, but feels her stony, unforgiving, not yet ready to respond.

In Ilona's firmament he is the sun, the moon, the stars and comets. In the zip pocket of her satchel she has the postcards he has sent her from Japan and Hong Kong and Phnom Penh, since he has been away, every single one.

*

Back in the Nice flat, the celebrations go on as they must when the starring princess seems to have assumed for the duration an expression of fixed hostility, and made her body stiff as an angry cat, resisting arms placed round her shoulders, squeezes at the waist. Brigitte has manoeuvred Daniel out of the kitchen so Ilona can finish her cake, but the giggles and good humour of the preparations have evaporated in Ilona's glare. Her stomach is twitching, now, with a nagging nerviness she hadn't had time to feel for the moment of Daniel's return. This is to her like a bad dream of someone you love acting in some unaccountable way, when you know it is really that person, but there's some feature out of place, some bizarre incongruity. She can feel hatred in her eyes and cannot force out, much as she would like to, more than a snarl.

At table, conversation is brittle. Ilona, long before the appearance of her splendid cake, has got up and slammed into her room. Daniel lets pass an interval calculated to suggest treating her exit respectfully while being sufficiently brief to rule out indifference.

He knocks. 'Pussycat?' She is sitting at her desk in the corner by the window, apparently absorbed in homework, pressing out purposefully and angrily with a pencil the outline of a map, and fails, very obviously, to look up. Daniel senses that some ritual is needed, some ceremony, some way back in. Surprising Ilona, followed so quickly by the party, was apparently not, he thinks, a good idea, but he could hardly have turned them out, these people who have kept his ward, and the apartment, together through his absence, these people, whom, after all, he loves, and who love him, he and his almost-daughter... . He sits down in the armchair behind her, and inquires neutrally from this oblique angle, 'Lots of homework?'

She shakes her head, but doesn't turn round. He tries something more frontal: 'I've missed you.'

'You didn't have to go.' Her voice seems older, harsh and uncompromising in a way he does not remember. In the moment in which she says this, she also cancels it by twisting out of her chair and snaking into his lap, arms shooting around his neck; but he has had time to feel a need to win her over of a different nature, has seen her as something other than a child.

When this embrace, innocent enough, has spent itself, they go back to the kitchen and dinner finally takes the course that was originally intended, with exclamations of admiration over the cake, laughter and photographs, as the wrapping paper builds up among the winebottles and candlesticks. Ilona rushes off again to her room to try on the oriental dress Daniel has brought her, in deep turquoise embroidered satin, and is photographed again with her hair twisted up by Brigitte over a pencil, sitting on Daniel's knee, smiling over the ruins of the cake with half the world still on it.

*

Later, when they are alone, he caresses her along her fine cheekbone, as she stands, still in her dress, hair beginning to fall out of its pins, like some parody of an eastern princess, the right age, the wrong colour, so pale, so blonde. He does not take her on his lap like a small child, as before, because he wants almost to throw her onto her rosy bed, quietly but urgently, rucking the narrow dress up over her thighs, excited by the knowledge that this would have the effect of holding her legs closed in a satin sheath, locking him out.

He wants to thrust his hand under her skirt, hear the satin rip, loudly, have his hand just fit, there, between her thighs, curl round; his fingers softly cupping the curve of her pubis, plump among her bony sharpness, and to feel her intensely wet, hear her breath coming in little sighs, her heart racing. In all this, he cannot see her face.

Faint with desire, eyes closed, his hand still in her hair, he hears her say, 'What's the matter?' Her small interrogative forefinger traces his nose, lips, chin.

'Nothing,' Daniel tells her, opening his eyes, concentrating, pulling himself together. 'You know I love you very much.'

Ilona does not yet have the words to say, There is something else to know.

He takes her to bed with him that night because he cannot leave her, and much later, when the dawn has almost broken, she wakes up in a spreading pool of wetness of a different kind, and they are back to the routine; papa comforting the little girl for whom everything has been too much, not tears before bedtime, but a little accident before the night is through. She has woken confused and uncomfortable and has to be comforted and reassured. They go back to sleep, Daniel's hand resting in the small of her back as she curls into him, as if in absolution.

*

If Daniel is tempted by this unfallen Eden, this sensual delight of a lifetime, days later he thinks, involuntarily and with an ugly start, of the little girls he had seen in the East, and some of them were no more than little girls, made to display themselves behind plate glass, bold and coquettish or demure and virginal, according to the proprietor's whim and the known tastes of the punters. One of his lawyer partners in Bangkok had told him that because virginity was prized or at least priced so highly, it was not unusual for the girls to be taken to the hospital after their first time and sewn back up. She and her colleagues managed, she said, to save some of them, to get them out, to trace their families and see them on the road to some sort of a normal existence. They had sat in silence, in the splendid restaurant of the Bangkok Oriental, thinking of the others.

XXVII

'Ilona.' Daniel stands with her between his knees in her bedroom facing the mirror at the foot of the rosy bed. 'You know why you have to go away.'

Silence. He strokes the inside of her left elbow, waits.

Her cases are packed and piled in the hall.

'It's just for a while, Lili. My sweet, my baby. Just until we sort things out. I'm – sorry. I really am.'

His hands are inside her top. He kneads the flawless skin over the fragile ribcage, the tips of his thumbs joined in the dip of her spine, and thinks he would rather be dead than be without this child. He rests his face against her shoulder, smells her hair, brushes her neck with his lips. Still she does not speak.

'You understand why you have to go?'

'No.' A whisper. He strokes her hair. 'We never did anything wrong.'

'When you're older,' he tells her. 'When you grow up, you'll understand. Nothing stays the same, my darling.'

'I'm still the same,' she says, holding his eyes in the mirror. 'Daniel, I'm still the same.' And she turns and climbs onto his lap, straddling him, burrowing into his chest. In his solar plexus he has an actual, physical pain.

She says it again, running back to him at the airport on the brink of departure, locking her arms around his neck, and his tears fuse with hers as he pushes her away.

'It's just for a while, my love,' he tells her. 'Just a while. Everything's going to be alright. I promise.'

Like some rooted thing being dug out of my heart, thinks Daniel, as he watches her leave for the second time.

Epilogue

Not to be able to move on, not to be able to go back, and in the final analysis, not to be able to stay the same... . Impossibility dispenses with Ilona, she implodes in upon herself, disappears; and Daniel goes one day to the airport to meet her return flight, and waits, and hears a suppressed gasp run round the crowd and sees a faint, desperate swaying set in around him, as up on the arrivals board clicks the number of her flight, followed by four Xs, in a neat row. That plane will not be coming in to land. No-one can suspend the flow of time; there are no little girls frozen in perfect moments.

Life comes with no return ticket. You can go where you like, but to return to where you came from is not an option. And all the emergency exits are alarmed. All you can do is go on and away, but go back, never. This is why Munch's embryo-man is screaming. My novel is my scream.

And so it ends, for now. The rest is perhaps a lifetime's rearranging.

* * *

I sleep and the sky is heavy with light. I am in a boat, a pleasure boat; there is to be a trip to a small island visible in the distance. I have invited you, but the question is, will you come? Finally you arrive, but you sit yawning. Every so often you disappear from view, but you always come back. I feel I could enjoy this trip if only I could get rid of all these people, weighing the boat down and obscuring the view.

Then suddenly the cumbersome steamer has turned into a punt: I am back in Durham, trailing along the river, with Daniel visible as shadow on water and you beside me. We are all equally ageless, we are the quintessence of ourselves. Everything is preternaturally bright, the spaces between things oddly large. I am possessed by lightness. I ask, 'Where are we going?' And, staccato, amused, even a little alarmed, the answer comes from Daniel:

'God knows!'

189

And we glide away, into the indigo light.

I realise you have left the boat, and are walking along beside us on the towpath. Your face is at its most beautiful, radiant. I look up at you, and you wave, once, twice: goodbye. There are no words.

I desperately want to ask, I have to ask, You won't forget me? But nothing comes out. I can feel the boat sliding silently downstream.

I awake.

Or, I never awake from this dream.

'Where are we going?'

– 'God knows!'

You have taught me how to live, how to die. I wrote this for you, my chosen father, before I wrote it for myself.

This is to you and for you; a book accidentally left out of a suitcase, irrevocably forgotten in the depths of a luggage locker on a long-deserted station.

For a full list of our publications please write to

Dewi Lewis Publishing
8 Broomfield Road
Heaton Moor
Stockport SK4 4ND

You can also visit our web site at

www.dewilewispublishing.com